MUDDLE EARTH
BOOK ONE
ENGELBERT THE ENORMOUS

Paul Stewart &
Chris Riddell

*Illustrated by Paul Stewart &
Chris Riddell*

First published in 2003 by
Macmillan Children's Books Ltd
This Large Print edition published by
BBC Audiobooks by arrangement with
Macmillan Children's Books Ltd 2005

ISBN 1 4056 6086 4

British Library Cataloguing in Publication Data available

Printed and bound in Great Britain by
Antony Rowe Ltd., Chippenham, Wiltshire

For Anna and Jack

NAME: Joe Jefferson
OCCUPATION: Schoolboy
HOBBIES: Football, TV,
arguing with his sister
FAVOURITE FOOD:
Anything not cooked by
Norbert

NAME: Randalf the Wise
Muddle Earth's leading
wizard
OCCUPATION: Um . . .
Muddle Earth's leading
wizard
HOBBIES: Performing spells
(I think you'll find that's
spell!—Veronica)
FAVOURITE FOOD:
Norbert's
squashed tadpole fritters

NAME: Henry
OCCUPATION: Joe's dog
HOBBIES: Walkies,
chasing squirrels, sniffing
strangers' bottoms
FAVOURITE FOOD:
Dog food, obviously

NAME:
Norbert the Not-Very-Big
OCCUPATION: Ogre
HOBBIES: Thumb-sucking,
cooking—especially cake
decorating
FAVOURITE FOOD:
Everything

NAME: Veronica
OCCUPATION: Familiar to
the great wizard, Randalf
the Wise
HOBBIES: Being sarcastic
FAVOURITE FOOD:
Anything not cooked by
Norbert

NAME: The Horned Baron
OCCUPATION: Ruler of
Muddle Earth and husband to
Ingrid
HOBBIES: Ruling, and doing
whatever Ingrid tells him
FAVOURITE FOOD: Bad-
breath porridge

NAME: Dr Cuddles
(Sshhh! Don't
say his name out loud!)
OCCUPATION: (SSHHH!
No one even knows he exists!
HOBBIES: (Didn't you hear
what I just said?)
FAVOURITE FOOD:
Snuggle-muffins

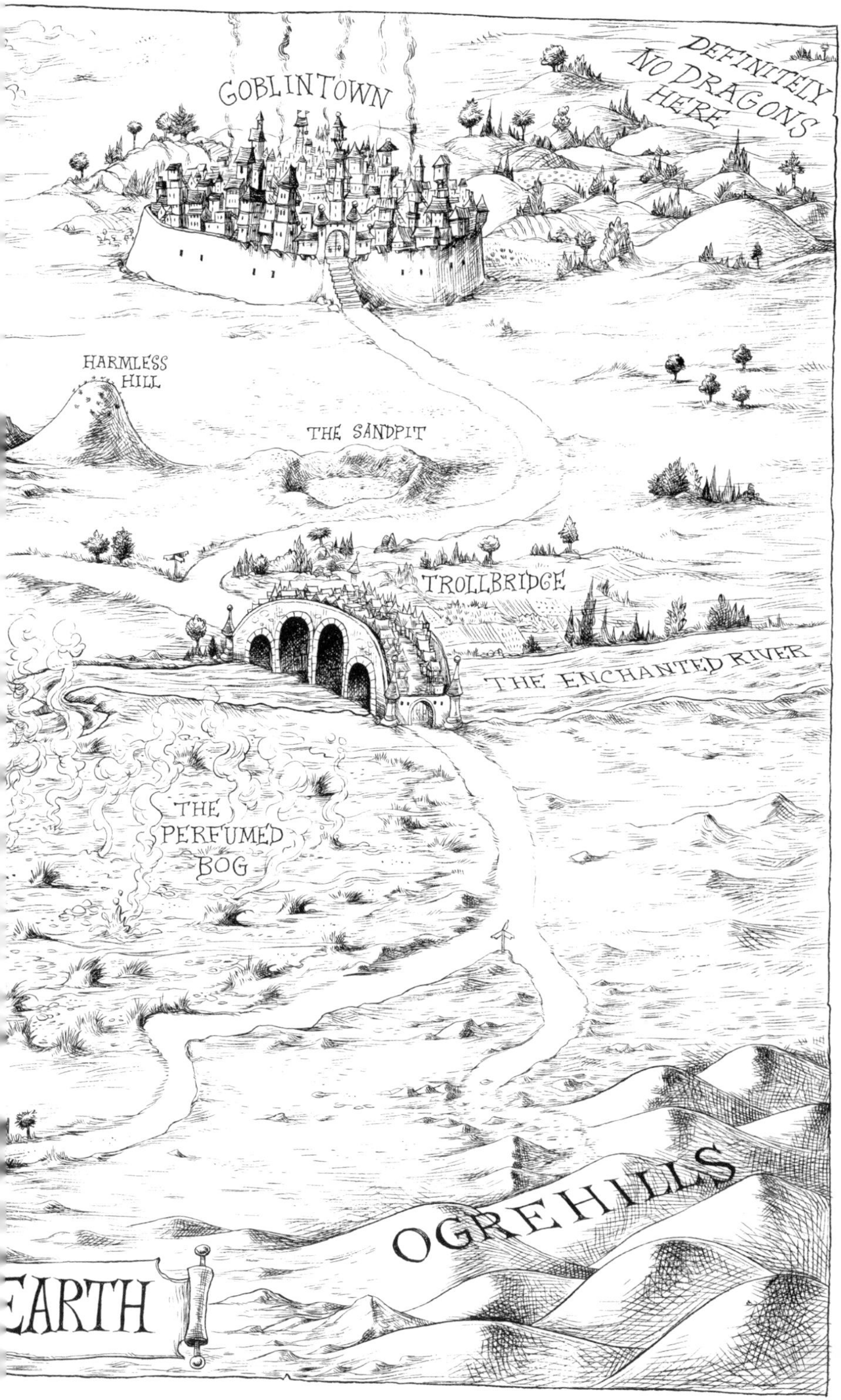

GOBLINTOWN

DEFINITELY NO DRAGONS HERE

HARMLESS HILL

THE SANDPIT

TROLLBRIDGE

THE ENCHANTED RIVER

THE PERFUMED BOG

OGRE HILLS

EARTH

Book 1

ENGELBERT THE ENORMOUS

Prologue

Night was falling over Muddle Earth. The sun had set, the sky was darkening and already two of its three moons had risen up above the Musty Mountains. One of these moons was as purple as a batbird. The other was as yellow as an ogre's underpants on wash day. Both were full and bright.

The land was full of noises as the day creatures (such as tree rabbits, hillfish and pink stinky hogs) said goodnight to the night creatures (such as stiltmice,

3

lazybirds and exploding gas frogs), who were just getting up. High above their heads, the batbirds had left their roosts and were soaring across the purple and yellow striped sky. As they bumped into each other, the air filled with their characteristic cry: *'Ouch!'*

In Elfwood, the trees bowed and bent as a chill wind howled through their branches. In the Perfumed Bog the oozy mud bubbled and plopped. In the far-off Ogrehills, there was the slurping sound of a thousand thumbs being sucked and a thousand sleepy voices murmuring *'Mummy!'*

Twinkling lights were coming on throughout overcrowded Goblintown and, as the goblins prepared their evening meals, the air was filled with the smells of bad-breath porridge and snotbread—and the sounds of too many cooks.

'Have you spat in this?'

'No.'

'Well, go on then, before I put it in the oven.'

By contrast, Trollbridge was cloaked in cold, dank darkness. The trolls who lived there could see nothing of the cabbages and turnips they were eating for supper. Their deep voices rumbled up from their dwellings beneath the bridge.

'Has anyone seen my mangel-wurzel?'

'It's over here.'

'*OW!* That's my head!'

As the purple and yellow shadows swept down from Mount Boom to the Horned Baron's great castle below, a loud, piercing voice ripped from the windows of the highest tower. Another of the inhabitants of Muddle Earth seemed to be finding it hard to tell the difference between a root vegetable and a head.

'Walter, you turnip-head! WALTER! Where *are* you?'

It was Ingrid, wife of the Horned Baron himself, and she was far from happy.

'Coming, my sweet,' he called out as he climbed the circular stairs.

'I've just seen something I really want in this catalogue,' Ingrid continued. 'Singing curtains. It says here, "No self-respecting Horned Baron's wife should be without these enchanted window hangings to lull her gently off to sleep at night and sensitively wake her with song the following morning." *I* want to be lulled to sleep by singing curtains, Walter. *I* want to be woken with song. Do you hear me?'

'Loud and clear, love-of-my-life,' the Baron replied wearily. 'All *too* loud and clear,' he muttered under his breath.

The next moment the third moon of Muddle Earth—a small, bright green sphere which only seemed to appear when it felt like it—sailed up in the sky to form a perfect equilateral triangle with its yellow and purple neighbours. The three moons lit up the Enchanted Lake, which hovered high up above the ground, and the seven magnificent houseboats bobbing about on its glistening waters.

Six of the houseboats were dark and deserted. The seventh was bathed in an oily, orange lamplight. A short, portly individual by the name of Randalf was staring out from one of its upper windows at the configuration of coloured moons. A budgie perched on his balding head.

'Norbert,' he said at last to his assistant. 'The astral signs are auspicious. My pointy hat, if you please. I feel a spell coming on!'

'At once, sir,' said Norbert, his voice gruff yet well-meaning. As he stomped across the floor to the wizard's cupboard the whole houseboat dipped and swayed. Norbert the Not-Very-Big was a fairly weedy specimen, as ogres went—but he was still an ogre. And ogres, even weedy ones, are big and heavy.

'You feel a spell coming on?' said the budgie, whose name was Veronica. 'No, don't tell me. It couldn't be the spell to summon a warrior-hero to Muddle Earth by any chance?'

'It might be,' replied Randalf defensively.

Veronica snorted. 'Some wizard you are,' she said. 'You've only got one spell.'

'Yes, yes, don't rub it in,' said Randalf. 'I do the best I can. With all the other wizards . . . *errm* . . . away, I've got to hold the fort.'

'This is a houseboat, not a fort,' said Veronica. 'And the other wizards aren't *away*, they're—'

'Shut up, Veronica!' said Randalf sharply. 'You promised never to mention that dreadful incident again.'

The houseboat lurched once more as Norbert strode back across the room. 'Your pointy hat, sir, he said.

Randalf placed it on his head. 'Thank you, Norbert,' he said, trying hard to overcome his irritation with

Veronica. She was *such* a know-it-all! Why couldn't he have had something nice and sweet for a familiar like an exploding gas frog or a slimy bog demon? True, they might have been a bit smelly, but at least they wouldn't have answered back all the time. Not like this infernal budgie. Still, he was stuck with Veronica now, and he'd just have to do what he always did in these situations—make the best of it.

He carefully removed a piece of paper from the folds of his cloak, delicately opened it up and cleared his throat.

'Here we go,' came a muffled voice from under his hat as Randalf began to recite the incantation from the piece of paper. *'Hail, oh Triplet Moons of Muddle. Shine down on these Words of Enchanting now I utter . . .* um . . .'

'That's all very well and good,' Veronica's voice broke in, 'but it's the last bit you need to concentrate on.'

'I know that,' Randalf muttered through clenched teeth. 'Be quiet now. I'm *trying* to concentrate.'

'That'll be a first,' Veronica

commented, wriggling out from under the brim of the hat.

Randalf stared down at the spell miserably. Much as he hated to admit it, Veronica was right. He *did* need to concentrate on the last part of the spell. The trouble was, the bottom of the piece of paper had been torn off, and with it, the all-important words of enchantment for the warrior-hero-summoning spell. Once again he would have to improvise.

'Creator of Wonders, Master of Intricate Arts, Possessor of Breathtaking Skills . . .' he began.

'Don't overdo it,' Veronica cautioned. 'You said something like that last time you summoned a warrior-hero. Do you *want* another Quentin the Cake-Decorator?'

'No, you're right,' said Randalf. He rubbed his beard thoughtfully. 'All right,' he said at last, 'how about this?' He took a deep breath.

'Strong . . . and loyal . . . and . . .' He gave Veronica a dark look. *'Hairy. Oh, Triplet Moons, on these words shine clear. Let a mighty warrior-hero*

now appear!'

There was a bright flash, a loud crash and clouds of purple, yellow and green smoke billowed from the fireplace. Randalf, Norbert and Veronica spun round and stared, open-mouthed—and beaked—at the figure which appeared amidst the thinning smoke.

'What is *that*?' said Norbert.

Veronica squawked with amusement. 'I've just got one thing to say,' she chuckled. 'Come back Quentin the Cake-Decorator, all is forgiven!'

'Shut up, Veronica!' said Randalf, 'and stop sniggering. Everything's going to be fine! Trust me, I'm a wizard.'

Joe slammed down his pen angrily and clamped his hands over his ears to shut out the surrounding din.

'This is hopeless!' he bellowed. 'Hopeless!' The noise was coming in from all directions—above, below, the room next door . . . It was like being stuck in a giant noise-sandwich.

On the desk in front of him, the title of his English assignment—'My Amazing Adventure'—headed a blank piece of paper. It was early evening at the end of a sunny midsummer Sunday, and if Joe was to get the homework finished and ready to hand in on

Monday morning then he needed to get down to work. But how *could* he, with that infernal racket going on all round him?

Joe Jefferson lived in a small brick house with his mum, dad, older sister, younger twin-brothers and his dog, Henry. To a casual observer, the Jeffersons  seemed like a nice, quiet family. It was only when you stepped in through the front door that it became clear that they were anything *but*.

Mrs Jefferson worked in a bank. She was tall, slim, dark and fanatically house-proud. Mr Jefferson—a travelling sales-rep by day and a DIY freak at night, weekends, holidays and any other spare hour he could find—was short, stocky and never more happy than when clutching a power tool in his hands.

Over the years, Mr Jefferson

had constructed a garage, converted the loft, knocked rooms through, put up shelves and cupboards, built a conservatory, landscaped the garden and was currently working on a kitchen extension. At least, that was what *he* would say. So far as Mrs Jefferson was concerned, the thing her husband was best at was making a mess.

At this precise moment the electric drill was busy battling it out with the vacuum cleaner as Mrs Jefferson followed Mr Jefferson around the kitchen—attachment pipe raised high like a light-sabre—sucking up the dust from the air before it had a chance to settle.

As the noise vibrated up through his bedroom floor, Joe shook his head. He'd never get his homework done at this rate, and if he didn't, he'd be in serious trouble with Mr Dixon.

He wondered wearily why his dad didn't take up a nice quiet hobby—like chess, or embroidery—and why his mum couldn't be just a little less obsessed with cleanliness. And why his sister, Ella, who had the converted attic-room above his head, had to do everything—from flicking through a magazine to putting on mascara—to the accompaniment of loud, pounding music. And why the twins' favourite game was chasing-up-and-down-stairs-screaming.

Joe opened the drawer in his desk, pulled out his earplugs and was just about to shove them into his ears, when Henry let out a bloodcurdling howl and started barking furiously.

'That's it!' Joe yelled. He leapt up from his desk and stormed across the room. 'Henry!' he called. 'Come here, boy.'

The barking grew louder. It was coming from the bathroom. So were Mark and Matt's squeals of delight.

'He's in here, Joe,' they shouted.

'Henry!' Joe called again. 'Heel!'

Henry came bounding on to the landing and stood in front of Joe, tail wagging and tongue lolling. The twins appeared behind him.

'He was drinking the water from the toilet bowl again,' they shouted excitedly. 'So we flushed it!'

Joe looked down at the water dripping from Henry's hairy face. 'Serves you right,' he laughed.

The dog barked happily and held out his paw. Upstairs, Ella's door opened and the music grew louder than ever. Ella's angry voice floated down.

'Shut that dog up!' she yelled.

From downstairs, the sound of the electric drill was abruptly replaced by loud hammering.

'Come on, boy,' said Joe. 'Let's get out of this madhouse!'

He turned and, with Henry at his heel, went down the stairs, grabbed the lead from the hook by the door and was just about to leave when his mum noticed him.

'Where are you going?' she shouted out above the sound of the vacuum cleaner and hammer.

16

'Out,' Joe replied. He opened the door.

'Out where?'

But Joe had already gone.

The local park was deserted. Joe picked up a stick and threw it for Henry, who chased after it, retrieved it and dropped it back at his feet for another throw. Joe grinned. However exasperating his life became, he could always count on Henry to cheer him up. He ruffled the dog's ears and tossed the stick a second time, then set off after Henry.

Across the grass they went, past a cluster of trees and down the hill. As they approached the stream, Joe whistled for Henry to return and clicked the lead into place. If Henry ended up splashing about in the dirty water again, his mum would go mad!

17

He patted the dog's head affectionately. 'Come on, boy, we'd better get back. That essay won't write itself.' He turned to go. *My Amazing Adventure,*' he muttered. 'What a stupid title . . . Henry, what's wrong?'

Henry was standing stock still, the hairs along his back on end and his ears and nose twitching.

'What is it, boy?' Joe knelt down and followed the dog's intent stare.

Henry strained on the lead and whimpered.

'What can you see?' Joe muttered. 'Not a squirrel, I hope. You know what happened last ti . . . *aaargh*!'

Unable to remain still a moment longer, Henry suddenly bounded forwards. Head down and following his nose, he dashed straight for a massive rhododendron bush, pulling Joe along behind. The good news was that Henry was heading for a hole in the dark foliage. The bad news was that the hole was only dog-height.

'Henry! Henry, stop!' he shouted and tugged in vain at the lead. 'Stop! You stupid . . .'

The rest of the sentence was lost to a mouthful of leaves as Joe was dragged into the bush. He ducked down and tried his best to shield his eyes with his free hand as Henry dragged him deeper and deeper inside.

All at once, the branches and leaves began crackling with silvery strands of electricity, the air shimmered and wobbled and filled with the sound of slow mournful music—and the smell of burnt toast.

'What on earth . . .' Joe gasped as, the next moment, he was pulled headlong down into a long flashing tunnel. The music grew louder. The smell of burning became stronger and stronger until . . .

CRASH!

'Aargh!' yelled Joe. He was still falling, only now he could feel the sides of the tunnel grazing his elbows and bashing his knees as he continued to drop. And it was black—pitch-black. Joe cried out in fear and pain and let go of the lead. Henry disappeared below him. What seemed like an eternity later, he tumbled down out of the long vertical tunnel and landed with a heavy thump on the ground.

Joe opened his eyes. He was sitting on a tiled floor, bruised, dazed, surrounded by a thick cloud of choking dust and without the faintest idea what had just happened.

Had he fallen into a hole beneath the bush?

Had he cracked his head on a branch so hard he'd knocked himself silly?

As the swirling dust thinned, Joe found himself in a fireplace behind a huge pot, which was suspended on chains. He peered out into a dimly lit and exceedingly cluttered room.

There were tables against every wall, each one covered with pots, papers and peculiar paraphernalia. There were stools and cupboards and bookcases stacked high with boxes, bottles and books. Every inch of the walls was taken up with shelves and cabinets, maps and charts and countless hooks laden with bundles of twigs, roots and dried plants, dead animals and birds and shiny implements that Joe couldn't even begin to guess the purpose of. As for the floor, it was crowded with bulging sacks, earthenware pots and various angular contraptions made of wood and metal, with springs, pistons and cogs—and in the middle of all the chaos, two individuals with their backs turned.

One was short and portly, with bushy white hair and a blue budgie perched on the brim of his tall pointy hat The other was hefty, knobbly and so tall that he had to stoop to avoid knocking his head against the heavy chandelier above his head.

'He doesn't say much, sir,' the hefty, knobbly one was saying.

'Obviously the strong, silent type, Norbert,' the portly figure replied.

'Unlike Quentin the Cake-Decorator,' said the budgie.

The portly one bent down. 'Now, don't be shy,' he said. 'My name's Randalf. Tell us your name.'

Joe climbed to his feet. This wasn't happening. You don't take your dog for a walk one minute, fall into a bush the next and end up in somebody's kitchen. Do you? Joe closed his eyes and shook

21

his head. Where was Henry, anyway?

Just then, the dog emitted a short, sharp bark.

'Rough?' said Norbert, puzzled. 'Did he say "Rough", sir?'

'Yes, Rough!' replied the short character, nodding enthusiastically. 'Of course. An excellent name for a warrior-hero, being both short and to the point.' He leaned down and added conspiratorially, 'Rough the Strong? Rough the Slayer? Rough the . . . Hairy?'

Henry barked again.

'Henry!' Joe called.

The dog appeared from behind Norbert, tail wagging furiously, and bounded over to the fireplace. Joe bent down and hugged him tightly. It was so good to see a familiar face, even if this was a dream.

'Who are *you*?' came a strident voice.

Joe looked up and stared back at the two individuals staring at him. The short one had a bushy white beard. The tall one had three eyes. Both of them were standing stockstill, eyes (all five of them) wide and mouths agape. It was the budgie who had spoken.

'I said, who *are* you?' it demanded.

'I . . . I'm Joe, but . . .' he began.

'Don't you see, Veronica?' Randalf exclaimed. 'That must be the sidekick,' he said, pointing at Joe. All good warrior-heroes have a sidekick. Mendigor the Mendacious had Helispawn the goblin, Lothgar the Loathsome had Sworg Bloodpimple . . .'

'Quentin the Cake-Decorator had Mary the poodle,' Veronica muttered.

'Shut up, Veronica,' Randalf snapped. 'You'll have to excuse my familiar,' he explained to Henry. 'She's been getting a bit big for her boots recently.' He turned to Joe. 'I'm right, aren't I? You are Rough the Hairy's sidekick. His sword-carrier, perhaps? Or his axe-sharpener?'

'Not exactly,' said Joe, in a dazed sort of voice. 'And his name is Henry, not Rough. I was holding his lead when . . .'

'So you're his *lead*-bearer,' Randalf interrupted. 'Joe the lead-bearer. Hmm. Unusual, admittedly, but not totally unheard of.'

The budgie, who was wearing small yet sturdy lace-up boots, coughed. *'I've never heard of it,'* she said.

'Shut up, Veronica!' he said, and brushed the bird off the brim of his hat. 'We're forgetting our manners,' he went on, turning back to Henry. 'Let me introduce myself properly. I am Randalf the Wise, Muddle Earth's leading wizard.'

'Only wizard, more like,' said Veronica, settling on his shoulder.

'And this,' Randalf went on without missing a beat, 'is my assistant, Norbert—or Norbert the Not-Very-Big, to give him his full title.'

'Not very big!' Joe blurted out in astonishment. 'But he's gigantic.'

'Taller than you or me, I grant you,' said Randalf, 'yet for an ogre, Norbert is a small and rather weedy specimen.'

'You should see my father,' said Norbert, nodding. 'Now he *is* gigantic.'

'But back to the matter at hand,' said Randalf. 'I have summoned you here, Henry the Hairy, great warrior-hero, to . . .'

'Warrior-hero?' Joe interrupted, 'Henry's not a warrior-hero. He's my dog!'

Henry wagged his tail and rolled over with his legs in the air.

'What's he doing?' said Norbert, his three eyes open wide and panic in his voice.

'He wants you to tickle his tummy,' said Joe, shaking his head in disbelief. 'Any minute now, I'm going to wake up in hospital with a big bandage on my head.'

'Go ahead, Norbert, tickle his tummy,' said Randalf.

'But, sir,' said the ogre weakly.

'Tickle!' said Randalf. 'And that's an order!'

As Norbert bent down, the room gave a lurch. He gently stroked Henry's tummy with a massive finger.

'Go on, go on,' said Randalf impatiently. 'He won't bite.' He smiled at Joe. 'It seems there's been a slight misunderstanding,' he said, stroking his beard.

'There's always a misunderstanding with you,' chirped the budgie.

'Shut up, Veronica. I was under the impression that Henry the Hairy was the warrior-hero I had ordered—strong, loyal and . . . errm . . . hairy. But if, as you say, he is in fact a dog, then *you* must be the warrior-hero . . .'

'He doesn't look very strong, or for that matter, very hairy,' said Veronica dismissively. 'If *he's* a warrior-hero, then *I'm* Dr Cuddles of Giggle Glade!'

'Veronica,' Randalf snapped, 'if I've told you once I've told you a thousand times *never* to utter that person's name in my presence!'

'Brings back memories, does it?' Veronica taunted, and flapped up into the air. Randalf tried to swat her.

'Ow, watch where you're flying,' Norbert shouted, taking a step back as the budgie booted him in the ear.

Joe clung on to the great hanging pot as the whole room seemed to tilt to one side.

'Button it, you great lunk!' Veronica shot back.

'You and whose army?' Norbert countered.

Joe watched in open-mouthed

amazement as the wizard, the ogre and the budgie rounded on one another angrily. This was absolutely crazy. Who were they? Where was he? And most important of all, how was he going to get home?

'It's . . . it's been lovely meeting you all,' he shouted, interrupting the three shouting protagonists, 'but it's getting late and I've still got my homework to do. I really should be leaving now . . .'

The three of them stopped mid rant, carp and criticism, and turned to him.

'Late?' said Randalf.

'Leaving?' said Norbert.

Veronica jumped up and down on the wizard's head, feathers all fluffed up. '*You're* not going anywhere!' she squawked.

'Ouch!' cried Joe, rubbing his arm.

'Again, sir?' asked the three-eyed ogre, bending over him.

'No, three times is quite enough,' said Joe ruefully.

There's nothing quite like an ogre pinching your arm to convince you that you're not in a dream, and Joe was now totally convinced that this was no dream. But if it wasn't, then where on earth was he? And how had he got there? Henry wagged his tail and licked the ogre's hand.

Before Joe had a chance to ask any questions, the clock on the wall above the fireplace erupted with insistent noise. There was coughing, the sound of a tiny throat being cleared and fists and boots battering on a small wooden door which suddenly

sprang open. A little elf—dressed up in grubby looking underpants and with a length of elastic tied around its waist—jumped out and dived into mid-air.

'Five of the clock!' it screeched as it reached the end of the elastic, before rebounding and disappearing back inside the clock with a muffled crash.

'Five?' said Randalf wearily. 'But it's dark outside.'

30

The door sprang open a second time and the elf popped its head out. 'Or thereabouts,' it said, and disappeared again.

'Wretched clock's slow again,' Randalf grumbled. 'The mechanism probably needs cleaning.'

'I should say so,' said Veronica scathingly. 'Judging by the state of those underpants.'

'Shut up, Veronica!' said Randalf.

' "Shut up, Veronica!" ' said Veronica. 'That's your answer to everything. Well, I won't shut up! Call yourself a wizard. You've only got one spell—and you can't even do that properly.' She flapped her wing at Joe. 'I mean, look at him,' she said. 'Is it just me or is our so-called warrior-hero a little on the short side? Not to mention puny— and gormless. And as for his hairy sidekick . . .'

'*Shush*, Veronica,' said Norbert, patting Henry on the head. 'You'll hurt his feelings.'

Henry wagged his tail.

'Ooh, look, his waggler's waving!' Norbert cried. 'Does he want his

31

tummy tickled? Does he? Does he?'

He jumped up and down excitedly. The room lurched backwards and forwards alarmingly, and more books and utensils clattered to the floor.

'Norbert!' said Randalf, sternly. 'Behave yourself! Remember what happened with Mary the poodle. You don't want that to happen again, do you?'

Norbert stopped jumping, and shuffled to the corner of the room.

'Very nervous animals, poodles,' said Veronica, who was perched on Randalf's head. 'Ruined the carpet!'

'Shut up, Veronica!' shouted Randalf. 'That's all in the past. We have a new warrior-hero here and he'll be fine.' He clamped a hand on Joe's shoulder. 'Won't you, Joe? Just the job for the Horned Baron's purposes. Once he's kitted out . . .'

'Kitted out?' said Joe. 'What do you mean, kitted out? I don't want to be kitted out. I just want to know what's going on,' he added angrily.

'Temper, temper!' said Veronica.

'The fiery disposition of a warrior-hero,' said Randalf. 'Excellent!'

'What *are* you talking about?' Joe asked. 'I've got to get back for tea. And I've got this essay. I haven't even started yet . . .'

'Tea? Essay?' said Randalf smiling. 'Ah, yes. The mighty deeds of a warrior-hero—the great tournament of tea, the epic slaying of the monster essay! Of course you must get back for these tasks, but first, if you could just lend a hand with a tiny little task we have here . . .'

'I can't!' Joe insisted. 'I've got school tomorrow. I must get back. If you brought me here, you can send me back.'

'I wouldn't bank on it,' Veronica muttered.

'I don't think you appreciate the difficulty involved in summoning a warrior-hero from another world,' said Randalf solemnly. 'I mean heroes don't just grow on trees—well, apart from those in the Land of Hero-Trees that is. It's a long and painstaking process, I can tell you, by no means as easy as you seem to believe.'

'But—' Joe began.

'For a start, the three Muddle moons must be correctly aligned—and that doesn't happen often. If we'd missed this evening's triangular configuration, there's no knowing how long we'd have had to wait for the next one.'

'But—'

'Furthermore,' Randalf went on, 'because of a slight technical hitch with the actual spell—'

'What he means is, he's lost half of it,' said Veronica.

Randalf ignored her. 'You're only the second hero I've actually successfully summoned. The first one was Quentin—'

'The one with the poodle and the kilo of icing sugar,' Veronica butted in.

Joe became aware of a soft sniffing sound and looked up to see three big fat tears rolling down from Norbert's bloodshot eyes and over his lumpy cheeks. 'Poor, dear Quentin,' he sobbed.

'Cry baby!' Veronica mocked.

'Oh, but he never stood a chance!' Norbert wailed.

'That's enough, you two,' said Randalf.

'Sorry, sir,' said Norbert. He wiped his nose on the back of his sleeve, but kept sniffing.

'As I was saying,' said Randalf. 'First there was Quentin, and now I have summoned you . . .'

'But you had no right!' shouted Joe. 'I didn't ask to be summoned! I didn't ask to be pulled through a hedge, down a tunnel and into this, this . . . junk room!'

'Damn cheek,' came a muffled voice from the clock.

'I didn't ask to be kitted out by a stupid wizard! And insulted by a stupid budgie! And pinched by a stupid three-eyed ogre!' stormed Joe.

'Actually,' said Norbert. 'You did ask to be pinched. You said, "Pinch me. If this is a dream then . . ."'

'SHUT UP!' shouted Joe. 'SHUT UP!'

Norbert jumped back, his eyes wide with terror. 'Oh, help!' he bellowed. 'Mayday! Mayday!' And he jumped up as high as the ceiling would allow,

35

crashing back down on to the floor with both feet a moment later.

The room keeled to one side. Randalf fell, Veronica flapped up into the air, while Joe was catapulted across the room.

'Aaaaaargh!' he yelled as he hurtled past Randalf and Veronica and crashed into the wall opposite, missing the open window by a fraction. Dazed and winded, he slid to the floor. The room continued to roll back and forth, back and forth.

'Norbert, you bird brain!' shouted Randalf.

'How dare you!' screeched Veronica. 'Bird brain indeed!'

Randalf sighed as the room gradually righted itself. He turned to the ogre. 'Say "sorry" then,' he told him.

'I'm sorry, sir,' said Norbert miserably. 'Very, very sorry.'

'Not to me, Norbert,' said Randalf. Norbert frowned with confusion. 'To our guest here, our warrior-hero,' Randalf explained. 'To *Joe*,' he said, and pointed towards him.

'Joe!' Norbert cried out in horror. He saw him lying on the floor. 'Did I do that?' he said. 'Oh, I *am* sorry. So, so very sorry.' Tears welled up once again in his eyes. 'It's just that I panic when someone shouts at me. I have a very nervous disposition. In fact I was almost called Norbert the Wet-Trousers instead of Norbert the Not-Very-Big, because—'

'Yes, yes,' said Randalf. 'Pick him up, Norbert. Brush him down.'

'Yes, sir. At once, sir,' and he hurried back across the room.

Joe, by this time, was already climbing to his feet quite successfully on his own. As Norbert came lumbering towards him, the boat lurched again. Joe stumbled towards the open window.

'What on earth?' he exclaimed.

Randalf pushed past Norbert and placed his hand on Joe's shoulder. 'Not quite,' he said. 'Welcome to *Muddle* Earth.'

Joe stood stock-still as he stared out of the window. He was barely able to believe what his eyes were telling him.

37

For a start, instead of the one familiar white moon in the sky, there were three: one purple, one yellow and one green. And the landscape! It was like nothing he'd ever seen before, with vast areas of fluorescent green forest and glistening rocky wasteland—and far in the distance, tall, smoking mountains.

Most curious of all, however, he realized that he wasn't underground at all, but rather in some kind of a boat. And there were others. Five . . . six

others, all bobbing about on a lake which . . . But no, it made no sense. He closed his eyes, then opened them again.

There was no doubt about it. The lake was suspended high up in the air, without any means of visible support.

Joe turned to Randalf. 'The lake,' he gasped. 'It's . . . it's floating . . .'

'Of course it is,' said the wizard solemnly. 'The Enchanted Lake was raised up by the wizards of Muddle Earth many, many moons ago, and for

a very good reason—only no one can remember what that was. Anyway, they raised it . . .'

Joe frowned. 'But, *how*?'

'By great magic,' said Randalf solemnly.

'And *that's* something you don't see round here much these days,' Veronica chipped in.

'Magic?' said Joe softly. He shook his head. 'But . . .'

'Don't you worry about it, young warrior-hero from afar,' said Randalf. 'You've got a lot to learn. Thankfully, I am an excellent teacher.'

'Yes, and I'm an exploding gas frog!' Veronica retorted.

'Shut up, Veronica!' said Randall.

'There you go again,' said Veronica huffily, and turned her back on the proceedings.

'As I was saying,' Randalf continued. 'I shall teach you everything you need to know for the small task which lies ahead.' He smiled. 'Things are going to work out well this time, I can feel it in my bones. Joe, here, will see us proud.'

Veronica sniffed. 'I still don't think

he looks like much of a warrior-hero,' she said.

'He soon will,' said Randalf. 'We'll set off for Goblintown just as soon as day breaks.'

Just then the elf sprang out of the clock. 'Half past twenty-six, and that's my final offer!' it shrieked.

'*Yip! Yip! Yip! Bibbitty-Bibbitty!*' came a shrill voice. 'This is your early morning wake-up call: *Boing!*'

Joe's eyes snapped open, just in time to see the elf disappearing back behind the little wooden doors of the clock.

Joe looked round, and groaned. Everything was exactly the way it had been when he'd curled up in his hammock the night before. The clock, the room full of junk, the floating lake . . . What was more, it was still dark.

'What time do you call this?' Randalf demanded, emerging from the far end of the room.

The door of the clock flew open. 'Early morning!' snapped the elf. 'Or thereabouts: The door slammed shut.

'What's going on?' squawked Veronica. 'I've only just tucked my beak under my wing.'

Norbert lumbered out of the shadows, yawning and stretching. 'Is it morning?' he said.

Randalf looked out of the window. There was a fuzzy glimmer of light on the horizon. High in the sky the noisy purple batbirds were soaring back to the woods, to spend the day resting upside down at the top of the highest jubjub trees. 'Almost,' he said.

'Stupid clock,' Veronica muttered.

'I heard that!' came an indignant voice from the clock.

'Never mind all that,' said Randalf. 'We're awake now, so we might as well make an early start. Come on, Joe. Stir your stumps. Today's your big day.' He turned to the three-eyed ogre. 'Norbert,' he said. 'Prepare breakfast.'

'Are you sure I can't tempt you with any more?' said Randalf, ten minutes later.

'No, thanks,' said Joe.

'You'll need to keep your strength up,' Randalf persisted.

'Such as it is,' added Veronica unkindly.

Joe looked at the ladle of slop hovering above his bowl. 'I'm really full,' he lied.

Without any doubt, Norbert had produced the strangest breakfast Joe had ever eaten in his life—lumpy, green porridge that tasted of gooseberries, a small cake iced with love-hearts and a mug of foaming stiltmouse milk.

'But you haven't touched your snuggle-muffin,' said Norbert, looking hurt.

'I'm saving it for later,' said Joe. 'It looks lovely, though.'

The ogre sighed. 'Dear Quentin taught me everything I know. He was an artistic genius with icing sugar.'

'Right, then,' said Randalf, clapping his hands together. He stood up and grabbed his staff. 'Let's get this show on the road.'

Relieved, Joe jumped up from the table, grabbed Henry by his lead and followed Randalf downstairs. Norbert stomped down after them.

'Eager to get started, eh, Joe?' said Randalf warmly. 'An excellent sign for a warrior-hero. We've summoned a good'un this time, Veronica.'

'You said that about Quentin,' the budgie was not slow in reminding him. 'And look how that turned out.'

'We must not look to the past,' said Randalf as he opened the door. 'But to the future.'

He stepped outside. Joe followed him, still none the wiser about what exactly was going on. He *seemed* to be on the lower deck of a houseboat, but it was difficult to know for certain.

Underneath the vessel, fat fish swam round and round in the crystal clear water. They reminded him of the goldfish at home and, for a moment, he thought that perhaps it wasn't so crazy here after all.

High above him, small fluffy purple clouds scudded across the sky. Below him—and attached to the side by a rope—was a small boat. At least that's what Joe thought at first. It was only as he stepped across from the rope ladder to the bobbing vessel that he realized it was not a boat at all, but a bathtub. Joe clapped his hand to his forehead.

'What was I expecting?' he said to

himself 'Of *course* it's not a boat. After all, this *is* Muddle Earth.'

The bathtub gave a wild lurch as Joe stepped into it. Henry jumped in beside him.

'Not there,' said Veronica. 'You sit at the other end where the taps are.'

'If you don't mind,' said Randalf, climbing in and sitting down. 'Just watch your head on the shower attachment if it gets a little bit . . . *errm* . . . choppy.'

'It *always* gets choppy with Norbert in charge,' said Veronica. 'You've sunk two boats, one wardrobe and an inflatable mattress. Now we're using our last bathtub. It'll be the kitchen sink next!'

'Shut up, Veronica!' said Randalf. 'Come on, Norbert. We're all waiting.'

The ogre climbed into the bathtub, which wobbled about dangerously on the water. Kneeling down, Norbert seized two objects from the bottom of the bath. One was an old tennis racquet, the other was a frying pan. He leaned forwards and began paddling furiously.

The bathtub reared up in a great

47

swell of spray and froth, and sped across the surface of the lake. Norbert's arms were like pistons; up down, up down, up down they went. The edge of the lake came closer. Joe gasped.

'We're going to fall off!' he shouted.

'Trust me, I'm a wizard,' said Randalf. 'A little further left, Norbert,' he told the ogre. 'That's it.'

Joe looked up. He saw that they were heading for a waterfall.

'Hold on tight and watch out for that shower attachment,' the ogre smiled, and paddled faster than ever.

Closer and closer the waterfall came, louder and louder grew the sound of the raging torrent spilling over the edge.

'This is crazy!' Joe yelled.

'True,' said Randalf. 'But it's the only way down. Trust me, I'm a . . .'

'I know,' Joe muttered as he gripped the sides of the bathtub with white-knuckled ferocity, 'you're a wizard.'

'One last paddle should do it!' Randalf shouted.

Norbert obliged. For a moment, the

bathtub see-sawed up and down at the very edge of the lake. Joe gasped as Muddle Earth opened up before him in a broad, panoramic view.

'Brace yourselves!' came Randalf's voice above the raging cascade as the bathtub toppled over the edge. 'Here we go . . . *o-o-o-oh*!'

Veronica screeched. Henry howled. Joe screwed his eyes tightly shut. Only Norbert seemed to be enjoying himself.

'*Wheeeee!*' he cried as the little bathtub

with its five occupants hurtled down the roaring, foaming torrent of water.

The wind whipped past so fast, Joe could barely breathe. Stinging water slapped his face. His head pounded, his heart was in his mouth, his grip was slipping . . .

SPLASH!

The bathtub struck the pool at the bottom of the waterfall with colossal force.

It sank.

It rose.

It bobbed around on the surface like a ball, until the current swept it down into the relative calm water of the river beyond. Joe opened his eyes.

'That was . . . terrifying,' he gasped.

Veronica snorted. 'You wait until the return journey,' she said.

'We've taken on water!' Randalf announced. 'Quick, Norbert, start bailing!'

Norbert looked down at the water swilling around the bottom of the bathtub. He picked up the frying pan, then paused. 'Don't worry, sir!' he said, reaching down into the water. 'I'll save us!'

'No, Norbert!' Randalf shouted. 'Remember last time!'

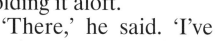

Too late. The ogre had already yanked out the plug and was holding it aloft.

'There,' he said. 'I've let the water out, sir!' He paused, and stared incredulously at the fountain of water gushing up from the plughole. 'Oops!' He looked up at Randalf. 'I've done it again, haven't I, sir?'

'I'm afraid so,' said Randalf.

'Abandon bathtub!' Norbert shouted.

With a gurgle and a plop, the bathtub abruptly disappeared beneath them. Joe kicked his legs, and headed for the nearest shore, with Henry doggy-paddling by his side. The pair

of them dragged themselves up on to the bank. Veronica, who had decided to fly rather than swim, landed beside them, only to be soaked by a spray of water as Henry shook himself dry.

'Well, that's the last of the bathtubs,' she said. 'You'd think he'd have learned about plugs by now.'

Joe said nothing. The sight of the Enchanted Lake suspended in mid-air far, far above his head had left him speechless. As he watched, a fat silver fish dropped out of the bottom of the lake, fell down through the air and into the gaping beak of one of the waiting lazybirds clustered together beneath the lake.

Randalf and Norbert climbed out of the river, dripping with water. Norbert shook himself dry, drenching Veronica for a second time.

'Thank you very much!' she exclaimed indignantly. 'Now you're trying to drown me on dry land!'

'Sorry,' said Norbert meekly.

Randall looked up at the sun, which was now peeking over the distant mountains. 'No harm done. Quite refreshing in fact,' he said. 'Let's set off. With a brisk pace, we should arrive at Goblintown by midday.' He turned to the ogre. 'If you'd do the honours, Norbert, my good fellow . . .'

'Yes, sir,' said Norbert. He crouched down on his hands and knees.

With the budgie perched on his head, Randalf climbed on to one of the ogre's great, broad shoulders. He looked at Joe. 'Well, come on. We haven't got all day,' he said.

Joe climbed gingerly on to the other shoulder. 'Won't we be too heavy?' he said.

'Of course not,' said Norbert. 'I'm a two-seater. Now, my cousin Ethelbertha is a four-seater with an extra box-seat at the front and back . . .'

'Yes, yes,' said Randalf. 'If you're quite ready, Norbert.'

Norbert straightened up and climbed to his feet.

'Forwards!' ordered Randalf, and

tapped the ogre on the head with his staff. Norbert lurched into movement and strode off, with Henry trotting along by his side.

On her lofty perch, Veronica tucked her head beneath her wing. 'I always get ogre-sick on long journeys,' she said weakly.

They were following a track which ran parallel to the Enchanted River. It was clearly seldom used, and had become totally overgrown. Tall jub-jub trees lined both sides of the path, their bendy branches heavy with sleeping batbirds. Norbert brushed past them.

'Ouch! Ouch! Ouch!' they cried.

Joe couldn't believe he was riding to Goblintown on an ogre's shoulders. About now, he should have been handing in his essay. He ducked to avoid a jub-jub branch and, with a thud, a bat birdlanded in his lap. Of all the excuses for late homework, 'Sorry, sir, I was too busy riding ogres and dodging batbirds,' had to be the weirdest. How on earth *would* he explain this to his teacher?

'It'll be easier once we hit the road,'

said Randalf brightly. 'Not far now.'

'Liar,' muttered Veronica queasily.

By the time they did finally reach the road—or rather *roads*, since they had arrived at a three-way junction—Joe was feeling a little ogre-sick himself. Norbert had stopped at a signpost which stood by the side of the road.

To their right, according to the peeling gold lettering, was *Trollbridge (not very far)*. To their left was *Musty Mountains (quite a long way)* Joe craned his neck to check whether Goblintown was also marked. It was.

GOBLINTOWN (THIS WAY, A VERY LONG WAY AWAY, SO STOP LOOKING AT THIS SIGN AND GET A MOVE ON, STUPID.)

'Charming!' said Joe.

'Come on, then, said Randalf, tapping Norbert on the head. 'Let's get going.'

Norbert shuffled about awkwardly. 'Which way, exactly, sir?' he said.

'To Goblintown, of course,' said Randalf impatiently.

'I know *that*, sir,' said Norbert, staring at the signpost with a perplexed frown. 'But . . .'

'Norbert,' said Randalf, 'when I took you on as an official Wizard Carrier, you assured me you could read.'

'Believe that, you'll believe anything,' said Veronica.

'I *can*!' said Norbert. 'Little words, anyway.' He nodded at the signpost. 'These are all so long.'

Randalf breathed in sharply. *'This way,* Norbert,' he said. *'A very long way away, so stop looking at this sign and get a move on, stupid,'* he read.

'Who are you calling stupid?' Norbert muttered in a hurt voice as he set off. 'My cousin Ogred the Dribbler,' he said, his pace increasing, 'now he *was* stupid. Did I ever tell you about the time he got his head stuck in a . . .'

'Snuggle-muffin,' Randalf mumbled drowsily, his head suddenly lolling on his shoulders.

'Typical,' said Veronica. 'Sleeping like a baby again!'

'Sir always falls asleep when he's travelling,' said Norbert. 'And usually right in the middle of my best stories.'

'Can't imagine why,' said Veronica testily.

'Well, it must be tiring being a wizard,' said Norbert, 'what with all that reading and spells and stuff.'

'I suppose so: said Joe with a shrug.

'Oh, Randalf isn't a *real* wizard,' Veronica whispered into Joe's ear.

From up on Norbert's shoulders there came the sound of soft snoring.

'He isn't?' said Joe. 'But I thought . . .'

'Until the wizards—the proper wizards, the *Grand* Wizards—all disappeared, Randalf was just a lowly apprentice to Wizard Roger the Wrinkled,' Veronica explained in a hushed voice. 'It was only when they all went missing that Randalf started to pretend *he* was a Grand Wizard. He seems to have fooled the Horned Baron, but no one else is taken in. That's why he's so hard up. I mean, who wants to pay for the services of someone so useless?'

'Useless?' said Joe.

'Utterly useless!' said Veronica. 'Oh, the stories I could tell. The invisible ink that kept reappearing. The flying bicycle that fell to bits in mid-air. And all those poor goblins who ended up bald as an egg after trying his magic memory-cream. Not to mention Dr Cuddles.'

'Dr Cuddles?' said Joe. '*Who* is Dr Cuddles?'

'Only the baddest, meanest, most evil villain there ever was!' Veronica told him. 'He won't rest until he's the ruler of Muddle Earth, with everyone under his thumb. Randalf is in a right mess. He needs help.'

'And he's expecting me, as a warrior-hero, to sort all this out?'

'Good heavens, no,' Veronica replied. 'You're just here to earn Randalf some money, though if I were you—'

At that moment, a loud clattering, banging noise echoed through the air, cutting Veronica off in mid sentence. Joe looked up to see a flock of cupboards, their doors beating like wings, flying across the sky. 'What are *they*?' he gasped.

'They look like cupboards to me,' said Norbert.

'Do cupboards *normally* fly in Muddle Earth?' Joe asked, bewildered. He stopped and, with his hand shielding his eyes from the dazzling sun, peered into the distance. 'They're flying in formation—and they seem to be coming from that forest.'

'Elfwood,' said Veronica, nodding. 'That doesn't surprise me. There have been a lot of strange goings-on in Elfwood recently,' she added darkly. 'If you ask me, it's all to do with Doc—'

'*Aaargh!*' shouted Norbert as, still looking skywards, he failed to notice a large pothole in the road. He tripped, stumbled and crashed to the ground. Veronica flapped squawking into the air. Joe landed in a heap beside Henry.

Randalf rolled over in the dust.

'My lovely snuggle-muffin,' he murmured. 'I . . .' His eyes snapped open. He found himself sprawling on the ground. 'What's *happening*?'

'Please, sir. Sorry, sir,' said Norbert apologetically as he climbed to his feet. 'I tripped in that pothole.'

He pointed at a round hole in the road containing an upturned cooking pot and a mess of smelly porridge.

'Ruined!' said a small elf by the side of the road. 'Why don't you watch where you're going, you big oaf!'

'And why don't you watch where you're cooking!' squawked Veronica.

'What better place for a pot than a pothole!' the elf countered indignantly.

'Calm down everybody,' said Randalf, tucking his staff back under his arm. 'There's no harm done.'

The elf shrugged and, picking up the pot, strode off down the road. 'Wizards!' it snorted in a contemptuous voice.

The ogre leaned forwards, pulled Randalf up and began dusting him down vigorously.

'Easy, Norbert,' said Randalf. 'I don't know—soaked, dropped and now pummelled. This isn't what I'd call first-class travel.'

'No, sir. Sorry, sir,' said Norbert.

Randalf looked ahead. He called Joe to his side, and pointed. 'Over there,' he said. 'Just beyond that hill, you can see the spires of Goblintown peeking up. We are almost at our destination. You will be soon kitted out with the finest warrior-hero costume that money can buy . . .'

'Or rather, that you can *afford*, Veronica muttered under her breath.

As they approached the high wall that surrounded Goblintown, Norbert placed Randalf and Joe gently down on the ground. The noise from inside became louder and louder. There was shouting, hammering, wailing, whinnying, sawing, singing, ringing, bellowing, buzzing . . . all mixed up together in one tumultuous roar. And the smells!

Burnt tar, sour milk, wet fur, rotting meat—each one fighting to be noticed above the nose-wrinkling odour of unwashed goblins. Joe tried thinking of nice smells—chocolate, biscuits, strawberry ice cream . . .

'And I thought your socks were bad!' Veronica commented.

'Shut up, Veronica,' said Randalf. 'We don't want to hurt their feelings. Goblins can be very touchy.'

'*Humph!*' said Veronica. 'So far as I'm concerned, no one that smelly has the right to be touchy!'

'That's as may be,' said Randalf. 'Just remember, we're here on important business. So, button your beak!'

'Pardon me for breathing,' said Veronica huffily.

'By the way, my fine young friend,' Randalf added. 'I think Henry here is finding this pungent metropolis a little too exciting. Perhaps you'd better put your faithful battlehound on the lead.'

Sure enough, Henry's tail was wagging excitedly as his wet nose sniffed eagerly at the air. Joe clipped the lead into place.

They were now at the top of a tall flight of stairs before a set of huge wooden doors. Randalf seized the great knocker and hammered firmly against the wood.

Ding-dong!

Randalf turned to Joe. 'The goblins will have their little joke,' he said.

'Yeah,' Veronica chirped up. 'Like not letting us in.'

'Patience, Veronica!' said Randalf sharply. He looked at the door expectantly. Nothing happened. Randalf shuffled about, scratched his head, stroked his beard, rubbed his eyes. 'That famous goblin welcome,' he said at last. 'It's renowned throughout Muddle Earth.'

He knocked again, louder this time. *Ding-dong! Ding-dong! Ding-dong!*

The door flew open.

'I heard you the first time!' shouted a small, grubby, cross-eyed individual with gappy teeth and pointy ears. 'I'm not deaf!'

'A thousand, nay a million apologies, my goblin friend,' said Randalf, bowing low. 'Far be it for me to bring your hearing faculties into doubt. I merely . . .'

'What do you want?' the goblin scowled.

Randalf forced himself to smile. 'We wish to avail ourselves of your finest outfitting-emporium,' he said, 'with the express intention of purchasing your most—'

'You what?' the goblin said.

'We need to buy a warrior-hero outfit for the boy,' said Veronica, flapping her wing towards Joe.

'Leave this to me, V—' Randalf started to say. He was interrupted by the goblin.

'Well, why didn't you say so in the first place?' he snapped, opening the door for them all to enter.

'Shut that door!' shouted a voice. 'There's a terrible draught.'

'Take a deep breath everyone,' Randalf whispered over his shoulder.

'Come in, come in,' said the goblin impatiently. He slammed the door shut behind them. 'Welcome to Goblintown,' he intoned in a bored voice. 'The city that never sleeps.'

'Or washes,' muttered Veronica.

'Enjoy its many sights and sounds . . .'

'And smells,' said Veronica.

'And unique atmosphere.'

'You can say that again!'

'Veronica, I warned you!' Randalf

hissed. 'Will you *shut* up!'

'Have a nice day,' the goblin concluded, and yawned.

Joe screwed up his nose. 'Veronica's got a point, though,' he whispered. 'It really does stink here!'

'You'll soon get used to it,' Randalf told him. He turned to the goblin. 'Thank you, my good fellow. I'd just like to say what an honour, not to say, pleasure it is to . . .'

'Whatever,' said the goblin, and walked away.

Joe looked about him. Apart from the smell, Goblintown was amazing. Buildings had been built on other buildings, storey by storey, reaching up higher and higher. Teeming with life, the tall structures lined the maze of narrow alleyways on both sides. Joe looked up nervously as the great towering constructions swayed precariously back and forth. They looked for all the world as if they might topple over at any moment. What was more, since the buildings *were* so high, almost no sunlight penetrated to the alleys at the bottom.

Not that it was completely dark. Oil lamps hung from every building, bathing the bustling streets in a sickly, yellow light and filling the air with greasy smoke. The rank, burning fat joined the other disgusting smells of Goblintown: the foul odour of baking snotbread, the stale pong of unwashed bodies and the stench bubbling up from the drains.

'Follow me!' said Randalf. He pulled a baggy yellow item of clothing from his robes and raised it up high on the end of his staff.

'Are they what I think they are?' said Veronica.

'You never know when a pair of ogre's underpants will come in useful,' said Randalf, striding off. 'Keep your eyes on the pants everybody, and you won't get lost.'

Norbert sighed. 'I wondered where they'd got to,' he said.

'Now, Joe, pay attention,' said Randalf, 'You really must see the sights of Goblintown. On our right,' he announced, 'we have a typical goblin apartment. On our left, the Museum of

69

Moderate Achievements—while that,' he said, pointing up ahead to a particularly rundown building, 'is the Temple of the Great Verucca.'

'The Temple of the Great *Verucca*?' said Joe incredulously.

Randalf nodded. 'It is the site where Wilfred the Swimmer, that ancient goblin explorer, laid the first stone of what was to become Goblintown. Legend has it that he had been looking for a suitable place to build for seven long years when the pain from his great verucca finally forced him to abandon his search. He decided it was a sign. The rest, as they say, is history.'

'Spare us the guided tour!' squawked Veronica, fluttering overhead.

This way and that they tramped. Randalf was in the lead, with the yellow underpants held high, followed by Norbert, Henry—sniffing every street corner and straining at his lead— and finally, Joe. Goblins thronged the streets, shoving and jostling, arguing, shouting—and completely ignoring the strangers in their midst.

'Which is why,' Randalf concluded,

pausing to let the others catch up, 'we call Goblintown the Friendly City. It—*Ooof*!'

One goblin barged into Randalf. Another grabbed the underpants from the end of the staff and raced away through the crowd.

'My word!' shouted Randalf.

'My pants!' cried Norbert.

'Forget them,' said Veronica. 'We're here.'

As one, they all turned—and there, behind the windows of a particularly tall and ramshackle building, was a selection of shop-dummies, all dressed up in ornate warrior-hero costumes. Norbert stared at the gold letters on the sign swinging back and forth above the door.

'*Unc*...*Unc*...*Unc*...' he said.

'*Unction's Upmarket Outfitters*,' Randalf read for him. 'Well spotted, Veronica. Come on then, Joe. Let's get you kitted out.'

To Joe's surprise, they did not stay long in *Unction's Upmarket Outfitters*. Randalf led them up the aisle of the magnificent store—ignoring the tuts and sighs of the smartly dressed assistants as he went—to the very back. There, they climbed a broad curving staircase.

They emerged, not on the second floor of the outfitter's as Joe had expected, but in a different shop altogether. A brightly painted sign on the wall announced it as *Mingletrips Middle-of-the-Road Emporium*. The assistants, all of whom wore slightly plainer outfits, watched them suspiciously.

'I was looking for . . .' Randalf began.

'Yes?' said one of the assistants, his left eyebrow arched high.

'For the way up,' said Randalf.

The assistant nodded towards the far window. Joe frowned, puzzled. What were they meant to do there? Randalf, however, seemed unfazed.

'Ah, yes,' he said, and set off. The others followed him again.

Across the shop floor they went, out of the window and up a rusting circular staircase bolted to the outside wall.

They were greeted at the top with a third sign: *Drool's Downmarket Depot.*

'Keep up, we're nearly there,' said Randalf bossily. He began climbing an old wooden ladder propped up against the wall. 'And mind the eighth rung,' he called down. 'It wobbles a bi—'

'Aaargh!' Norbert cried out as the rung beneath his feet splintered and fell. He clung on tightly to the sides of the ladder, too frightened to continue.

'On second thoughts, perhaps it would be

73

better if you went back and waited for us there,' said Randalf. 'And look after Joe's battlehound,' he added.

Joe watched the quivering ogre slowly lowering himself back to the balcony. Then, somewhat relieved that he wouldn't have to carry Henry up the rickety ladder, he passed Norbert the lead.

'Be good, now,' he told the dog. 'All right?'

'All right,' Norbert replied meekly.

Taking extra care at the missing eighth rung, Joe scampered up the ladder. As he neared the top, he glanced down—and gasped.

Far, far below him, he could see the crowds of goblins streaming this way and that along the narrow alleys. Veronica fluttered down and hovered near his left shoulder.

'Come on,' she said encouragingly. 'Mustn't keep our know-it-all guide waiting.'

With his heart in his mouth, Joe completed the last few steps of the ladder. Randalf was there to meet him.

'Well done, lad,' he said. 'And

74

welcome to the finest outfitter's in all of Muddle Earth.'

'The cheapest, more like,' muttered Veronica.

There was a faded banner above the door. *'Grubley's Discount Garment Store,'* Joe read out—unable to keep the disappointment from his voice.

Just then, a gangly goblin with a large nose and filthy frilly apron appeared from behind them. 'Welcome,' he said.

'Thank you, *errm* . . Stink,' said Randalf, addressing the goblin by the name on his lapel.

'Actually, it's Smink,' the goblin replied.

'But—'

'Mr Grubley's handwriting,' the assistant said wearily. 'It's almost as dreadful as his dress sense.'

'Yes, where *is* old Grubbers?' said Randalf, looking round.

Smink shrugged. 'He said he had *business to attend to.*' He winced as if smelling something unpleasant.

'Did he now?' said Randalf. He turned to the others, smiling. 'I think everything is going to work out even better than I expected,' he whispered.

Smink had turned away and opened the door from the balcony into the store. Ducking down, he went in. Randalf did the same.

'Just as well Norbert did stay behind,' Joe muttered to himself as he stooped low. 'He'd never have got through this doorway.'

He straightened up to find himself in a room so messy, dark and grubby, it made the wizard's houseboat seem like a showroom.

There were boxes and bundles, bursting with materials, piled up against the walls, next to stacked shelving, stuffed with every conceivable type of boot and shoe. Huge, circular racks—some, three tiers high—creaked under the weight of countless garments, all sorted into different categories. Jackets and jerkins. Capes, cloaks and coats. Leggings and breeches. Jodhpurs and knickerbockers. Bodices, bustles and bibs. While high overhead, still more—in differing colours, sizes and styles—were suspended from large ceiling hooks.

'Oh, yes, sir, I can see the problem,' said Smink, fingering Randalf's cloak with obvious distaste. 'This one's totally threadbare. Shoddy workmanship, completely out of fashion and a hideous colour, if you don't mind my saying so.' He looked up. 'Wizard's cloaks are over here,' he said. 'Walk this way,' and he bustled through the shop with tiny, pigeon-toed steps.

'I couldn't walk that way if you paid me,' Veronica commented.

Smink turned. 'I'm sorry, did sir say something?' he asked.

'Actually, it's the lad we're here for today,' said Randal 'He needs kitting out as a warrior-hero. The full works.'

'I see,' said Smirk, looking Joe up and down and giving a sniff. 'That would be *battledress*, sir, which is right this way.'

As they all trooped across the floor to the far end of the room, pushing their way through the hanging mounds of garments, Joe felt the whole building swaying gently backwards and forwards. A pair of metal gauntlets fell to the ground with an ominous clatter.

'Well, they'll do for a start,' said Randalf. 'Next, a cloak.'

'The full works, you say, sir,' said Smirk. 'Might I recommend the leather Cloak of Impermeability. Fashioned by magic, it will deflect the blow of the mightiest sword.'

'Excellent,' said Randalf. 'Try it on, Joe.' Joe did so and inspected himself in a standing-mirror at the back of the shop. Randalf turned to Smirk. 'And headgear?'

'We have everything,' said Smirk with a wide sweep of his arm. 'Helmets—horned, winged, spiked or plumed; bonnets—war, jousting and . . . Ah, yes! A skull-faced shriek cap with matching ear pompoms—a bit of a speciality item, that one, sir.'

'I was thinking more of a standard sort of helmet,' said Randalf.

'Of course, of course,' said Smirk rubbing his hands together. 'Silly of me. What about this Helmet of Heroism. Very popular, sir. Very hard-wearing feathers.'

He removed a heavy bronze helmet

with five purple plumes, and placecd it on Joe's head. It fitted him like a glove.

'Sir will notice the tiny speakers concealed in the ear-rim. They play invigorating marching music as the warrior-hero strides boldly into battle.'

'Just the job,' said Randalf eagerly.

'And there are other matching accessories,' said Smink. 'The Shield of Chivalry, the Breastplate of . . . of . . . of Bravery and Perseverance, the Gaiters of Gallantry—to go with the gauntlets you have already so wisely chosen. And last, but not least, the Sword of Superiority,' he announced as he handed the final item to Joe.

'The Sword of Superiority,' said Randalf, sounding impressed. 'I'll take it. I'll take the whole lot,' he said.

'An excellent choice, if I might say so,' said Smink.

Joe looked at himself in the long mirror, and raised the sword high in the air. It looked quite convincing. He grinned. 'Not bad,' he thought. 'Not bad at all.'

'Sir looks fabulous, if I might be so bold,' said Smink. 'And not only that. These items all come with the Grubley Heroic Quest Success Guarantee—or your money back.' He returned his attention to Randalf and smiled an oily smile. 'Which brings us to the delicate matter of payment.'

'Ah, yes,' said Randalf. 'Payment.' He smiled back confidently. 'Old Grubbers knows how good my credit is,' he said. 'He told me to stick it all on the slate.'

'He most certainly did not,' came a gruff voice behind him. '*Never ask for credit, 'cause a refusal sometimes offends,*' it continued, getting louder with every word. 'So what cheeky so'n'-so is pretending I did?'

A stocky, bandy-legged individual with hairy ears and one thick, dark eyebrow, burst out of a rack of petticoats and pantaloons. 'You!' he said, fixing Randalf with a penetrating glare. 'I might have known!'

'Grubbers!' Randalf exclaimed, and went to shake hands.

'It's Mister Grubley to you, *Randy*,' he said, striding past the wizard's outstretched hand and tapping Joe on the shoulder. 'You can get that lot off for a start.'

Reluctantly, Joe removed the armour. Grubley turned to Randalf. 'Let me see. You still owe me for the last one. Quentin the Golden, wasn't it? One sparkly cloak, a pair of patent-leather bootees and the golden swan helmet with pink fur lining. It's cash or nothing from now on! Let's see what you've got.'

Hiding his irritation, Randalf reached into his cape pocket and pulled out a small leather pouch. He opened the top and poured a collection of coins into his palm. 'Eight muckles, five groats and a silver pipsqueak,' he said.

Grubley seized the tiny silver coin and bit into it. 'Hmm,' he said. 'Seems like we *can* do business after all. The bargain-basement's upstairs,' he said, pointing to a rope ladder which led up to a hole in the ceiling.

Perched precariously on the roof of the discount store, the so-called basement was like a huge box on stilts. It was cold and draughty, and swayed alarmingly as the wind howled round its flimsy walls. Like the store they had just left, however, it was crammed full of items of clothing.

'That's the trouble with you wizards,' Grubley was saying. 'You come in here demanding my best stuff for your so-called warrior-heroes and then they go out and ruin it all by getting squashed by an ogre. I mean, this is quality merchandise.'

Veronica snorted dismissively.

'What does he mean, 'squashed'?' said Joe nervously.

'Goblins will have their little jokes,' whispered Randalf.

'Here.' Grubley pulled out a cloak made of sacking and decorated with a fake-fur trim, and handed it to Joe.

'Love the fur,' said Veronica sarcastically. 'It's really fetching.'

'And is it protected perhaps by the power of impermeability?' asked

Randalf. 'Or the hex of deflection?'

'Not exactly,' said Grubley. 'Though I daresay it would make a wound sting a bit less. Probably.'

'We'll take it,' said Randalf.

Other items followed. The Woolly Gloves of Determination. The Cardigan of Optimism. The Wellies of Power. Joe tried them all on. It was when they came to the helmet that he finally spoke up.

'I'm not wearing *that*,' he said.

'Not wear the War-bonnet of . . . umm . . . Sarcasm?' said Randalf. He took Joe's arm. 'Notice how the helmet's round shape has been made to deflect blows from cudgels, truncheons, swords—and how here, at the front, an extra safety-feature has been attached. What's more, not only will the War-bonnet of Sarcasm protect your head, but it will also give the wearer the heroic ability to make rude comments about their opponents' dress sense and physical appearance.' Randalf took the helmet and placed it on Joe's head. 'Both in its workmanship and design,' he announced, 'it's a triumph!'

'It's a saucepan,' said Joe flatly.

'How astute you are,' Randalf said brightly. 'Indeed the helmet can also double as a cooking utensil—for those long expeditions, far away from home . . .'

'But . . .' Joe protested.

'Trust me, Joe,' Randalf interrupted. 'I know you are valiant and brave, but I could not in all conscience allow any warrior-hero to set forth on a quest without an enchanted helmet of such unique power.' He turned to Grubley. 'We'll take it,' he said. 'We'll take the lot.'

Grubley nodded, and began totting up the cost of the armour under his breath.

Randalf glanced through the window at the sun. 'It's getting late,' he said. 'We'll have to get our skates on.'

'Skates?' said Veronica. 'Don't you think the lad looks ridiculous enough as it is?'

'Shut up, Veronica,' said Randalf. He turned to Grubley. 'So, what do I owe you?' he said.

Grubley looked up. 'Eight muckles,

five groats and a silver pipsqueak, exactly,' he said.

Reunited at the bottom of the rickety ladder once more, Randalf, Veronica, Norbert, Henry and Joe made their way back down through the succession of clothiers and outfitters to the bottom of the tall, creaking building.

On every new level he came to, Joe found himself glancing into the mirrors—and each time he groaned. Dressed in the sacking cloak, the woolly gloves, the saucepan and armed with a dustbin-lid and a toasting fork, he looked a complete idiot.

As they emerged from the front entrance on to the street, several goblins stopped, turned, pointed and sniggered. Joe tugged at Randalf's sleeve.

'You've turned me into a laughing-stock!' he whispered in embarrassment.

'You can say that again,' Veronica laughed.

'Nonsense,' said Randalf. 'You look magnificent, Joe. Doesn't he, Norbert?'

Norbert nodded. 'I love the fur trim,' he said. 'And those silver buckles on his wellies are so sparkly!'

'He looks even worse than Quentin the Cake-Decorator,' said Veronica. 'And that's something I never thought I'd find myself saying. I mean, a toasting fork!'

Randalf looked up angrily. 'Toasting fork?' he exclaimed. 'Why you foolish bird. The Trident of Trickery is one of the finest weapons a warrior-hero could possess.'

'Oh, yeah!' said Veronica.

'It is!' Randalf insisted. 'How else could he launch a three-pronged attack on his enemy, eh? You tell me that.'

Veronica rolled her eyes.

'Trust me, Joe,' said Randalf. 'You

are the best warrior-hero I have ever summoned to Muddle Earth.'

'Which isn't saying much,' Veronica commented.

Norbert wiped a tear from his eye as he remembered the *other* warrior-hero Randalf had summoned.

'I have absolute confidence in you,' Randalf continued. 'And so will the Horned Baron, I'm sure.'

'But what does a warrior-hero actually have to *do* in Muddle Earth?' Joe asked.

For once, not even Veronica had an answer.

By the time they arrived back at the gates of Goblintown, it was already early evening. The cross-eyed guard stood up from his stool.

'Did you find the . . .' He noticed Joe and snorted with amusement. 'Ah, yes,' he said. 'I see you did.'

Back on board the ogre after a fitful night's sleep beneath the stars, Randalf instructed Norbert which way to go to get to the Horned Baron's castle. Turning right out of Goblintown, they followed a road which crossed a broad featureless plain towards the foothills of a vast mountain range. As they did so, the conversation turned to Joe's name.

'I mean, Joe isn't a *bad* name,' Randalf was saying doubtfully, 'but perhaps we should go for something a little more forceful, noble, impressive. In short, a more warrior-like name.'

'How about Joe the Terrible Toaster?' Veronica proposed. 'Or Josephine the Awfully Annoyed? Or what about Jo-Jo the Extremely Sarcastic . . . ?'

'Shut up, Veronica!' Randalf shouted. He turned to Joe. 'What about Joe the Barbarian? Short and to the point—and with just a hint of mystery. After all, with your Helmet of Sarcasm, Shield of Slight Protection and Trident of Trickery, you're a force to be reckoned with and no mistake. There isn't a dragon, ogre or whifflepook that wouldn't think very seriously before picking a fight.'

Joe stopped in his tracks. 'Dragon? Ogre?' he said. 'Are you seriously suggesting I should do battle with dragons and ogres?'

'And whifflepooks,' Norbert reminded him. 'Vicious, scaly little beasts, they are,' he said, looking round nervously.

'You're a warrior-hero, a barbarian, Joe,' said Randalf cheerfully. 'Savage blood courses through your veins. A stranger from a strange land, eager for adventure and utterly fearless!'

'Yes, well . . . Joe began, but a disgusting smell assailed his nostrils before he could finish. *Pfwooar!* What is that horrible pong?'

Norbert pinched his nose closed. 'De Busty Bountains,' he said.

'And mustier than ever,' said Veronica. 'Perhaps you should also have invested in a Clothes Peg of Destiny,' she said to Randalf. 'Our warrior-hero is looking a bit green.'

It was true. Joe was feeling decidedly ill. Although not as pungent as Goblintown, the warm, stale odour drifting in on the breeze from the Musty Mountains was quite disgusting —a stomach-churning mixture of mildew, mouse droppings and mothballs. As they rounded the corner, the mountains loomed up ahead of them. They were tall, jagged, forbidding and very, very musty.

'They stink!' Joe gasped.

'The Musty Mountains are extremely old, Joe,' said Randalf sharply. 'I daresay one day *you'll* be old and smelly yourself.'

'But—' Joe began.

'And how will *you* like it when everyone who passes you by tells you that you stink? Eh?'

Joe shook his head. Sometimes in Muddle Earth, there was simply no point arguing.

'Anyway, Joe,' Norbert added. 'Don't worry. You'll soon get used to it.'

On and on they went. Mile after mile. With Randalf and Veronica on one shoulder, Joe on the other and Henry trotting along by his side, Norbert strode unwaveringly onwards.

After several hours of going in a straight line, the road was becoming increasingly full of bends. It snaked its way through the valleys between the tall, jagged mountains. To Joe's surprise, Norbert was right; he did get used to the unpleasant smell. Or rather, what with everything else about him, he forgot all about it.

There were hairy squeak-moths that fluttered off as they approached, squeaking loudly. There were flightless scruff-birds which flapped about on the ground, chattering indignantly. There were odd thuds and spooky whooshing noises as rocks fell and the wind blew, and far in the distance Joe thought he heard an odd tinkly-tinkly sound.

When they came to a fork in the road, Norbert stopped. 'Which way, sir?' he said.

Randalf, who had dropped off for a few minutes, opened his eyes and looked round.

'The Horned Baron's castle, sir,' said Norbert. 'Should I turn right or left?'

'Left,' said Randalf.

'Where does the other road lead to?' asked Joe.

'Nowhere,' said Randalf. He tapped the ogre softly on the head with his staff. 'Proceed, Norbert,' he said.

Further on, as they rounded a sharp corner, Joe stared in awe at a chimney-stack-shaped mountain that loomed into view. Tall and imposing, it towered high above all the other mountains. From the crater at its top came little wisps of smoke which coiled up into the musty air and disappeared.

'What's that?' he asked.

The mountain let out a gentle, rumbling *boom* and a wispy smoke ring. Randalf, who had dozed off once more, grunted in his sleep.

'It's called Mount Boom,' said Veronica.

' 'Cause that's what it does,' added Norbert helpfully. 'It goes boom!'

Boom.

The feeble noise sounded again. It

was accompanied by a second smoke ring. The musty smell grew slightly mustier. This time, Randalf's eyes opened.

'Did I hear something?' he said.

'It was Mount Boom, sir,' said Norbert. 'Booming.'

'Excellent,' said Randalf. He rubbed his eyes. 'Then we are nearly there. The Horned Baron's castle should be just around the next corner. Charming location . . .'

'Apart from the smell,' added Veronica.

The road curved round to the left. Randalf pointed down through the musty, dusty air to a series of tall spires and turrets which peeked up above the line of jagged mountain-tops. 'There it is,' he announced. 'The castle of the Horned Baron.'

Norbert shuddered. 'The place gives me the creeps,' he said. 'It always has.'

'And as for the Horned Baron himself,' added Veronica. 'He can be so . . .'

Just then, the budgie's voice was drowned out by a loud rumbling sound which came from Elfwood. Joe turned to look. The tinkly-tinkly sound grew louder. The next moment, something curious emerged from the distant trees in a flurry of thick dust and sped towards them.

'Stampede!' Veronica squawked. 'Cattle stampede!'

At least that was what Joe *thought* she said. He squinted into the distance. 'Cattle?' he said. 'Are you sure?'

'Not *cattle*, cloth-ears,' said Veronica. '*Cutlery!*'

'Take cover!' Randalf cried as the stampede drew close.

Joe ducked down behind a rock and watched in amazement as the great herd of kitchen utensils pounded past. Knives, forks and spoons, ladles and tongs, scissors and skewers, peelers, sharpeners, crushers and mashers—all hurtling on in a wild and frenetic dash towards the Musty Mountains.

'There's definitely something afoot in Elfwood,' said Veronica darkly. 'Some strange, potent magic is brewing, you mark my words. And you know who's at the bottom of it. Doctor Cuddles . . .'

'Shut *up*, Veronica!' Randalf shouted crossly. 'How many more times must I tell you? That name is not to be mentioned in my presence under any circumstances.'

Joe frowned and turned to Veronica. 'But you said—'

'Shut up, Joe!' Veronica hissed. She turned back to Randalf. 'Don't you think we ought to get going?' she asked him.

'Quite so,' said Randalf. He

cautiously stood up and looked round. The cutlery had gone. 'Come on, then,' he said. 'It's safe to proceed.'

Inside the Horned Baron's castle at last, Randalf (with Veronica back on his head) led Norbert, Joe and Henry up a wide and winding staircase to the first floor. Randalf stopped at an imposing oak door.

'Wait here,' he instructed Joe, his voice echoing round the high vaulted ceiling. 'I'll introduce you to the baron when the moment is right. Timing is everything. Trust me, I'm a wizard.'

He turned and knocked.

'Enter!' came a loud, booming voice.

Randalf opened the door and went in. 'My Lord Horned Baron,' he said, and bowed low. Veronica hopped down on to his shoulder. Norbert curtsied. 'And how good it is to see his Lordship looking so well.'

A short, fussily dressed little man stopped his pacing and turned to Randalf. 'Oh, it's you again,' he said.

'Indeed it is,' said Randalf cheerfully.

The Horned Baron scowled. 'You're late!' he snapped. 'I sent for a wizard last Tuesday.'

'A thousand apologies for that, my Lord,' said Randalf, 'but you know how it is. One spell leads to another, and before you know it . . .'

'Indeed I do *not* know "how it is",' said the Horned Baron, his voice just a little too shrill and high-pitched. 'When I summon a wizard to the castle I expect him to drop whatever he's doing and come at once. Is that understood?'

'Absolutely, my Lord . . . Yes, my Lord . . . Sorry, my Lord . . .' Randalf babbled. 'I've been so busy. What with all the other wizards going . . . *umm* . . . on holiday . . .'

'Yes, well, I suppose you'll have to do,' the Horned Baron sighed. 'I've been at my wits' end! Apparently, there's a rogue ogre running amok. Great big brute of a thing it is. It's the last thing I need. What with all the rumours that something is not quite right in Elfwood.'

'Told you,' muttered Veronica smugly.

The mention of Elfwood turned Randalf a deep shade of red. 'An ogre, you say. What you need,' he went on hurriedly, 'is a warrior-hero.'

The Horned Baron groaned. 'That's what you said the last time, when I had that problem with the plumbing. What was his name? Quentin the Cake-Decorator? I'm still clearing up the mess he made.' He shook his head. 'The trouble is, the quality of the warrior-hero depends on the quality of the wizard who summons him, and quite frankly . . .'

His voice trailed away as he looked Randalf up and down, eyebrows raised and top lip curling. Randalf pulled himself up to his full height and puffed out his chest.

'The summoning of a warrior-hero involves hard work, prolonged study and utter dedication to the task,' he said. 'Only the most gifted wizards are able to carry out so demanding a spell. A wizard, I humbly suggest, such as myself.'

'*Humph,*' said the Horned Baron sceptically. 'We'll need more than a cake-decorator this time, Randalf. There's an angry ogre on the loose and his temper is getting worse by the day. According to my sources he goes by the name of Engelbert the Enormous. It's been absolute murder, I tell you. He's been ripping the thatch off cottages, trampling fields and orchards, *and* squeezing sheep . . .'

'Doesn't sound good,' said Randalf, and tutted sympathetically.

'He squeezed a whole flock only last night!' the Horned Baron went on. 'Something must be done!'

'And something *shall* be done!' Randalf announced. 'For I bear news that, after long and painstaking experimentation, I have managed to summon to Muddle Earth a great warrior-hero from afar. He is bold. He is brave. Sharp in intellect and valiant in battle. A warrior-hero whose reputation goes before him. A legend in his own lunchtime . . .'

'Get on with it!' said the Horned Baron irritably.

'Allow me to introduce, Joe the Barbarian!' Randalf said, and turned to the doorway expectantly.

No one appeared.

'Well?' said the Horned Baron. 'Where is he?'

'One moment, my Lord,' said Randalf, and cleared his throat. 'I give you . . .' He turned back to the door and bellowed at the top of his voice, 'JOE THE BARBARIAN!'

Before the echo had even died away, there came the sound of excited barking and scurrying claws, and Henry dashed into the chamber, ears flapping, tongue lolling and lead dragging along behind him.

The Horned Baron's eyes nearly popped out of his head. 'What in Muddle Earth is that?' he exclaimed. He turned on the wizard. 'Barbarian is right, Randalf!' he said sarcastically. 'Don't they believe in haircuts where he comes from?'

Randalf smiled. 'His Lordship has

misunderstood,' he said. 'This is not the warrior-hero of whom I spoke, but rather his faithful battle-hound.'

'Henry the Hairy,' Veronica murmured, and chuckled to herself.

'The real warrior-hero is about to enter,' said Randalf. 'Joe the Barbarian,' he announced again. His face creased up with irritation. 'JOE! Will you get in here. Now!'

Joe's pale face appeared nervously round the edge of the door. 'Did you call?' he said.

'He's not deaf, is he?' asked the Horned Baron. 'I don't give much for his chances if he is.'

'Of course he's not deaf,' said Randalf. 'That said, all the senses of this particular warrior-hero are so acute, so sensitive, so finely tuned that he could lose two or three and still remain completely invincible.'

Joe clattered into the chamber and stood next to the others. The Horned Baron glanced his way and sniffed dismissively 'He doesn't look up to much,' he said. He nodded towards Henry. 'Are you quite sure *he's* not the warrior-hero after all?'

'Appearances can be deceptive,' said Randalf. 'Take yourself, for instance. *We* know you're a great and noble Horned Baron, yet look at you . . .'

'What . . . what . . . what are you suggesting?' blustered the affronted Baron. 'I'm sure I don't know what you mean!'

Joe smiled nervously. For all his grand title and stately surroundings, the Horned Baron was, it had to be said, rather short. He was also weasel-faced, skinny and with scrawny arms and legs. Even his name was a bit misleading. Joe had assumed that the Horned Baron would have huge curling horns sprouting from the top of his head. Instead, he had to admit he was a little disappointed to see that the baron's name came from the oversized horns on his helmet, which kept slipping down over his eyes.

In short, the Horned Baron was a big let-down.

'What I meant, your Lordship, is this,' Randalf was saying. 'Your greatness and nobility are all the more impressive for being so . . . *well concealed.'*

'*Humph!*' snorted the Horned Baron, unsure how to take the wizard's words. He returned his attention to Joe and sighed wearily. 'I suppose that if this is all that's on offer, he'll have to do.'

Randalf smiled again. 'You know what they say,' he said. 'A barbarian in the hand is worth two cake-decorators in anyone's money.' He rubbed his hands together. 'And talking of money, if we could perhaps move on to the delicate matter of my fee.'

'Your fee?' asked the Horned Baron, his eyebrows arching alarmingly.

'Yes, two golden big 'uns, wasn't it?' Randalf ventured.

'Three silver pipsqueaks,' said the Horned Baron, jingling some coins in his pocket. 'And I'm being robbed blind!'

Randalf groaned. So little money to go such a long way. The trouble was, with his recent record, he was in no position to bargain. 'Three silver pipsqueaks it is,' he said and reached out for the money.

The Horned Baron abruptly withdrew his hand. 'But then, there was that incident with the exploding elf, wasn't there?' he said. 'I shall have to make a slight deduction. Oh, and then there's the matter of the melting silver goblet. And that terrible infestation of galloping green mould in the castle bathrooms . . . very nasty . . . In fact, after all the deductions, I calculate that *you* owe *me.*'

'But that's not fair . . .' Randalf began.

'Life isn't fair,' came the reply. 'Yet, for all that, I am a generous Horned Baron,' he said. 'Here, take this brass muckle.'

'You've got to stand up to him,' said Veronica.

'Shut up, Veronica,' Randalf hissed as, swallowing both his words and his pride, he pocketed the single coin. Who knows, perhaps his luck was about to change. Maybe Joe the Barbarian—warrior-hero *extraordinaire* —might just surprise him. He wouldn't count on it, but he'd just have to do what he always did in these situations and make the best of it.

'Go, then!' said the Horned Baron addressing Joe directly. 'Journey south, seek out Engelbert the Enormous and put a stop to his destructive behaviour once and for all. And when you have slain the fiend, I want you to bring me his head. There's a pouch of silver pipsqueaks for you when you do.'

'His head?' said Joe, horrified. *'Ugh!'*

'Just a figure of speech,' said Randalf hurriedly, as he seized Joe by the arm and steered him towards the door. 'Any proof will do.' He turned back to the Horned Baron. 'Consider it done, my Lord.'

Just then, the relative calm was destroyed by a heartstopping screech. *'WALTER!'*

Paling slightly, the Horned Baron smiled weakly.

'Walter! Where are my new singing

curtains? The ones I showed you in that catalogue. You promised me them ages ago. You're all talk, you are!' she shouted. 'I don't know, call yourself a Horned Baron!'

'It's all in hand, my little songbird,' he called back. 'I'm having them sent over. Made of the finest material, they are, and with the voice of an angel guaranteed. They're costing me the earth.'

'WAL-ter!' Ingrid screeched indignantly.

'But worth every last brass muckle, of course,' he hastily added.

Before the Horned Baron had a chance to remember precisely where his last brass muckle had actually gone, Randalf bustled the others out of the door, down the stairs and across the courtyard. He paused on the steps of the castle by the outer gate.

'All things considered,' he said, 'I think that went very well.'

'If being humiliated and swindled counts as doing well, then you're right,' said Veronica drily.

'Shut up, Veronica!' said Randalf.

He turned to Joe and clapped him on the shoulder. 'And so, Joe the Barbarian, the time is almost upon us,' he announced, trying to sound as cheerful as possible. 'We'll rest up here for the night. Then, as the sun rises over Muddle Earth tomorrow morning, so shall the quest begin!'

The following day dawned bright and early—unlike the day before, when it had been an hour late, and the previous Wednesday when it hadn't dawned until one-twenty in the afternoon. There were unconfirmed rumours flying about that Dr Cuddles was responsible. Whatever, on this particular morning the sun rose when it should—which was just as well, because if it hadn't, Randalf and the rest would have stood no chance of travelling to the Ogrehills in one day.

'Look lively,' Randalf said, several times, as he scuttled about getting everyone ready. Finally, they were off.

Swaying to and fro on Norbert's left shoulder, Joe was far from happy. Quite apart from the ogre-sickness which had returned with a vengeance the moment they'd set off, he was decidedly uneasy about the forthcoming quest.

'All this talk of ogres and squeezed sheep,' he was saying. 'I don't like the sound of it one little bit. I'm not a warrior-hero, I'm just an ordinary schoolboy—and I want to go home.'

Randalf leaned across from Norbert's right shoulder and patted Joe reassuringly. 'Don't worry,' he said. 'Everything's going to be just fine! Trust me, I'm a wizard.'

'That's easy for you to say,' said Joe. 'But look at the size of Norbert—and he's Norbert the Not-Very-Big! What on earth is this . . . this Engelbert the *Enormous* going to be like?'

'Enormous,' said Veronica. 'I think you'll find the clue's in his name.'

'Oh, I'm sure he is,' said Norbert. 'Absolutely massive! Twice as tall as me probably and three times as broad. In fact, Engelbert's bound to be even bigger than my grandfather Umberto the Unfeasibly Large—not to mention Uncle Malcolm Nine-Bellies . . .'

'Yes, yes, Norbert,' said Randalf. 'That's fascinating.' He turned back to Joe. 'The thing is, I don't expect you to actually fight Engelbert.'

'You don't?' said Joe.

'Of course not,' said Randalf. 'That would be ridiculous.'

'So what *do* you want me to do?' asked Joe.

'Psychology,' said Randalf, tapping the side of his head meaningfully. 'It's all about psychology.'

'It is?' said Joe.

'You see,' Randalf continued, stifling a yawn, 'as everyone knows, ogres are just great big softies. Isn't that right, Norbert?'

Joe clung on tightly as Norbert nodded in agreement.

'Really?' said Joe.

'Really,' Randalf confirmed sleepily. 'All you have to do is stride right up to him in your Wellies of Power, wave your three-pronged Trident of Trickery in his face, fix him with a stare from beneath your Helmet of Sarcasm and tell him to stop being so naughty, or else!'

'Or else, what?' said Joe.

'Or else you'll smack his bottom. Then you can make a really sarcastic remark about his appearance and he'll start blubbing like a baby. Simple.'

'If it's so simple,' said Joe, 'then why do you need me?'

'Psychology,' yawned Randalf. 'You're a warrior-hero. Ogres are terrified of warrior-heroes. They're giant-killers, dragon-slayers, troll-bashers —nobody stands a chance against a warrior-hero. It's a well-known fact!'

'But I'm not a warrior-hero,' said Joe. 'I keep telling you, I've never killed a giant or bashed a troll in my life. Honest!'

'In that costume, my lad,' said Randalf, shifting into a more comfortable position propped up against Norbert's right ear, 'Engelbert the whatever-his-name-is will take one look at you, burst into tears and promise to be a good ogre—especially if you say his eyes are too close together and he smells like a pink stinky hog. Trust me, I'm a . . .'

'Wizard?' said Joe. But Randalf was fast asleep. A soft, rasping snore fluttered through the air.

'That's him off again,' said Veronica. 'I've never known anyone sleep as much. Still, at least it shuts him up.'

'Shut up, Veronica,' mumbled Randalf in his sleep.

'Typical!' said Veronica.

They were returning the way they had come, back along the winding track through the Musty Mountains. Morning drifted slowly past, and soon it was early afternoon.

Boom.

Far far behind them, Mount Boom exploded softly. The hairy squeak-moths huffed to and fro looking for lost socks to eat, the scruff-birds rolled around in the musty dust by the roadside, while a swarm of rotund, antlered beetles buzzed slowly past, in search of killer daisies to pollinate.

'They look like miniature Horned Barons,' Joe laughed.

Veronica nodded, crunched her beak and swallowed. 'Only they taste better,' she said.

Joe winced and turned away. As he did so, he caught sight of something glinting out of the corner of his eye.

'What was that?' he said, looking down.

'What was what, sir?' said Norbert.

'That,' said Joe, pointing down at Norbert's left foot. 'Careful, don't tread on it.'

Sure enough, down by Norbert's left foot, glinting

in the half-light, a small silver teaspoon was doing what looked like a forlorn little dance in the dust. Round and round it was going, in ever-decreasing circles. Finally, the circles became so small that the teaspoon stopped in one place, did a last twinkling pirouette, and fell to the ground with a soft tinkly sound.

Joe jumped down and picked it up gingerly. As he held it, the teaspoon gave a little sigh.

'Did you hear that?' said Joe, holding it up. 'I think it gave a little sigh.'

'It's lonely,' said Norbert. 'It must have got separated from the herd in that cutlery stampede.'

'An enchanted teaspoon,' said Veronica darkly.

'Can I keep it?' said Joe.

'Finders keepers,' said Veronica. 'It'll go well with your saucepan and toasting fork.' She ruffled up her neck feathers and raised her beak. 'You can call it the Teaspoon of Terror—and terrify ogres with it!'

'Why have we stopped?' came

Randalf's voice. 'And did somebody mention tea?'

'I almost trod on a teaspoon, sir,' said Norbert. 'It could have been very nasty. My Auntie Bertha the Big-Footed was always treading on things. Or *in* things, more like. Why, that time she stepped in a great big dollop of—'

'Yes, yes,' said Randalf. 'Thank you, Norbert. Now, if you're quite ready, Joe, perhaps we should proceed. Our quest awaits us and we've still got a long way to go.'

Joe nodded and slipped the spoon into his back pocket. Norbert bent down, pulled him up on to his shoulder and set off once more. Randalf slumped forwards and drifted back to sleep.

It wasn't long before the road emerged from the highest peaks of the Musty Mountains and began winding its way through the foothills. These were as barren and musty as the mountains, and smelt strongly of old socks. To his right, Joe saw a tall, rounded hill he hadn't noticed at first. Unlike the other foothills, it was covered with thick grass and giant yellow and white daisies, their sweet scent perfuming the air. Stiltmice scampered through the verdant undergrowth; butterflies fluttered overhead. Joe breathed in the beautiful fresh air. He tapped Norbert on the shoulder.

'Not so fast, Norbert. Let's enjoy the view,' he said. 'What a lovely place! What's it called?'

Norbert shuddered anxiously, causing Joe almost to lose his balance.

'Careful!' he exclaimed. 'I nearly fell off just then! Oh, look, Norbert. Over there! How cute!'

A particularly appealing stiltmouse with big blue eyes was stepping daintily through the gently swaying grass, the aromatic breeze ruffling its white fur.

'That's Harmless Hill,' said Norbert.

'Harmless Hill!' Randalf woke up with a start. 'Norbert, my good fellow,' said the wizard. 'Why is it that whenever I wake up I find you standing still, gawping?'

'It's Joe, sir,' said Norbert apologetically. 'He wanted to enjoy the view.'

Just then, the stiltmouse gave a little cry as a daisy opened its gaping jaws and swallowed it whole. It gave an ugly belch.

'I thought it was called *Harmless* Hill!' said Joe, horrified.

'Oh, the hill's harmless enough,' said Veronica. 'It's the killer daisies you have to watch out for.'

Joe shook his head. 'This place is crazy,' he muttered. He looked down to check that Henry was still nearby.' 'Here, boy,' he called. 'Come up here with me, just in case there's a "perfectly safe" mountain up ahead, or a "don't worry, you'll be fine" meadow just round the corner.'

'I've never heard of those places,' said Norbert. 'But they sound terrifying!'

'Can we *please* get on,' said Randalf irritably. 'Wake me up when we get to Trollbridge.'

Norbert set off once again, this time at a brisk trot. Joe was getting used to ogre-riding by now, and with Henry safely in his lap, he relaxed. Slowly, his eyes grew heavy and his head began to nod.

The next thing he knew, Joe woke up with a mouth full of mud and Henry licking his face. He looked up. Randalf was on his feet, with Norbert fussing about him trying to brush down his robes.

'No, don't tell me,' Randalf was saying.

'Another pothole! You really should learn to look where you're going, Norbert.'

'It wasn't a pothole,' said Norbert tearfully.

'No,' came an angry little voice. 'It was a kettle hole actually—and my kettle is a complete write-off!'

An elf, who was standing in a small hole in the road, threw a flattened disc of metal, with what appeared to be a spout, down to the ground and marched off in a huff. Joe got to his feet, looked round and gasped. There in front of them was Trollbridge.

Built upon four great arches which crossed the river, the bridge was a solid, yet ornate, stone structure complete with tall pointy-domed turrets and magnificent gate-towers. Only when he looked more closely did Joe see just how neglected Trollbridge actually was.

'It's a bit grimy,' he said. 'And that tower looks as if it's about to collapse,' he added, pointing upwards.

Randalf shrugged. 'Trollbridge has a certain "lived-in" charm,' he said. 'Trolls have many fine qualities, but neatness is not one of them. Now stubbornness is another matter. Trolls can be very stubborn, as you'd know if you'd ever tried to get a troll to tidy its bedroom . . .'

'And they never throw anything away,' said Veronica, flapping her wing at the pile of junk at the foot of the gate-towers. 'I mean, look at all that mess!'

'Good day,' came a gruff, yet cheery, voice from the centre of the pile. 'Can I help you?'

There were bicycle wheels, taps, lengths of wood, screws and nails, nuts and bolts, coils of wire, a mangle, a bird cage, a washing-up bowl . . . and there, perched on a three-legged stool, a squat, bow-legged individual with tufty hair and rather ferocious-looking teeth sticking up from a protruding jaw.

'You certainly can,' said Randalf, stepping forwards. 'We wish to cross your magnificent bridge.'

'That'll be one mangel-wurzel,' said the troll.

'A mangel-wurzel?' said Randalf, and made a great show of searching through his robes. 'I'm afraid I'm fresh out of mangel-wurzels.'

'A turnip, then,' said the troll. 'You must have a turnip.'

'Not as such,' said Randalf.

'Then a carrot,' said the troll. 'Any root vegetable will do.'

'Sorry,' said Randalf.

'A potato?' he suggested. 'It doesn't matter if it's a bit mouldy.'

' 'Fraid not,' said Randalf.

The troll sighed. 'An onion? A courgette? A baby sweetcorn? All right then, I'll settle for a small dried pea.'

Randalf shook his head sadly.

'What sort of travellers are you?' said the troll. 'I mean, you haven't got a mangetout between you. I don't know,' he tutted. 'So what *have* you got?'

Randalf turned to Joe. 'I find myself in a somewhat embarrassing situation,' he said. 'I mean I've got my warrior-hero-summoning spell and a belligerent budgie, but that's about it . . .'

'You're *not* trading me!' squawked Veronica indignantly.

'Who'd have you?' snapped Randalf. 'Now, Joe. I don't suppose you . . .'

Joe rummaged round in the pockets of his jeans and pulled out an old bus ticket and a lolly stick. He held them out for Randalf's inspection.

'A chariot voucher from a far-off land,' said Randalf holding up the bus ticket.

The troll looked thoughtful. 'It's tempting,' he said. 'A far-off land, you say? Trouble is, I don't get out that much . . .'

'You surprise me,' said Veronica.

'Shut up, Veronica,' said Randalf, and he turned back to the troll. 'No? All right. Then how about this? A miniature paddle?'

'Miniature paddle,' said the troll, eyeing the lolly stick. 'Very nice, very nice. Lovely workmanship, but a bit— how can I put this? A bit on the small side.'

Randalf turned to Joe questioningly.

Joe pulled his front pockets inside out. 'Empty,' he whispered. 'I haven't got anything else . . .' As he spoke, he tried his back pockets, and there, nestling into the corner and stifling a sob, was the small silver teaspoon.

'There's this,' he said uncertainly as he held it up. 'The Teaspoon of . . . of . . . Terror!'

'The Teaspoon of Terror!' said Randalf, taking the spoon with a flourish. The spoon let out a timid little squeak.

Randalf ignored it. 'Forged by elves. Imbued with magic . . .'

'The Teaspoon of Terror,' said the troll, impressed, as Randalf laid it in his large, grubby hand. The teaspoon gave a sigh. 'Of course, a mangel-wurzel is the generally accepted fee, or a turnip. But you seem like an honest fellow . . . Oh, go on, then. A Teaspoon of Terror it is! Welcome to Trollbridge.'

'At last,' Randalf muttered. 'And thank you, once again,' he said as the troll opened the gate and waved them through. It's been a pleasure doing business with you.'

'As long as you remember, next time it's a mangel-wurzel or nothing,' said the troll as he strolled back to his stool.

Joe put Henry on his lead and followed Randalf and the others. It was market day in Trollbridge and the place was buzzing with feverish activity, for though the trolls lived under the bridge, their noisy bargaining, bartering and haggling was conducted up on top. A series of trapdoors sprang open and slammed shut constantly as the trolls hurried between the two. The balustrades on both sides of the bridge were lined with covered stalls and trestle tables, all laden with complete and utter junk, and run by enthusiastic trolls who were politely shouting out what wares they were selling.

'Old string! Do come and get your old string here! All lengths available.'

'I've the finest odd socks in Trollbridge if you'd care to take a look! Specially unwashed and aged by squeakmoths!'

'Mangel-wurzels! Please come and inspect my lovely mangel-wurzels!'

Boxes and sacks stood everywhere, each one filled with junk of all shapes and sizes, and the odd root vegetable.

'The trolls are renowned throughout Muddle Earth for their root vegetables,' Randalf explained. 'Especially their mangel-wurzels. They're passionate about their mangel-wurzels.'

'You don't say,' said Joe, as they passed by a rickety stall weighed down with a great pyramid of the things.

Slowly, they made their way across the great Trollbridge, the sound of the haggling and bartering ringing in their ears.

'I'll give you a jam jar of toe-nail clippings and a broken bucket.'

'Throw in the dried-pea rusk, and it's a deal.'

'Who will buy my sweet red gobstoppers? Sucked three times and dropped on the carpet . . .'

'Bottle tops! Bottle tops!'

'Bottle bottoms! Bottle bottoms!'

Joe stood, completely bewildered. There was so much to take in.

'Keep up, everybody!' Randalf shouted back impatiently from the end of the bridge. 'Norbert, put down that turnip. This is no time for eating. Come *on*, Joe. We haven't got all day.'

'Sorry,' Joe called back and, tugging Henry away from a display of amusingly shaped carrots, hurried to catch up.

'What kept you so long?' said Randalf.

'I was just interested,' said Joe. 'And everyone here seems so friendly and polite.' He frowned. 'But what do they do with all this rubbish?'

'The ways of the trolls,' Randalf

said, 'are as mysterious as they are bizarre . . .'

'In short,' Veronica butted in, 'he doesn't know. But you should see the state of their bedrooms!'

'Keep your voice down,' said Randalf, as they passed a second toll keeper at this end of the bridge. 'Trolls' feelings are easily hurt.'

The troll was identical in every way to the toll keeper at the other end— apart from his voice, which was high and shrill.

'Missing you already,' he squeaked.

With Randalf and Joe back on Norbert's shoulders, Veronica on Randalf's head and Henry trotting along behind, they continued on their way. Joe looked round and sighed as Trollbridge disappeared behind him. To his left was a broad and barren plain, to his right, a swampy bog.

All at once, Veronica let out a cry. 'Ogrehills ahead!' she shouted, her wing shielding her eyes from the low sun.

'Excellent news!' said Randalf with a yawn. 'We'll be there before we know it.' He turned to Joe. 'And you, Joe the Barbarian, will be able to prove your warrior-hero prowess once and for all.'

'Fantastic,' Joe mumbled. 'I can hardly wait. In fact . . His face suddenly screwed up. *'Pfwoooar!'* he groaned. 'What is *that* horrible pong?'

'Sorry' said Norbert. 'It must have been something I ate in Trollbridge.'

'Not you,' said Joe. 'I'm talking about that sweet, sickly smell.' It was like a pungent mixture of his dad's aftershave, his mum's aromatherapy oils, and his sister's cheap perfume, all mixed up with rotting vegetation. He held his nose. 'It's worse than the Musty Mountains!'

Veronica flapped her wings in front of her face. Henry whined miserably and rubbed his nose in the dirt.

'It's the Perfumed Bog,' said Randalf. 'I quite like the smell myself.'

'You would,' said Veronica.

'It reminds me of my beloved Morwenna,' he said dreamily. 'Morwenna the Fair, they called her . . .'

'Not behind her back, they didn't,' Veronica muttered. 'At least, not when

129

she grew that beard.'

'That was an accident,' said Randalf defensively. 'I was practising. Morwenna understood, even if her father didn't.'

'Morwenna! Morwenna! Let down your golden beard!' sniggered Veronica.

'SHUT UP, VERONICA!' shouted Randalf, very red in the face.

The further they went, the closer the road came to the Perfumed Bog, until the two were running along side by side, with only a thin line of stones separating them. Joe looked out across the swamp. Shrouded in pink mist, it was vast and flat, with giant lily pads and grassy tussocks, and dark pools of glistening purple mud which plopped and hissed as the perfumed gases bubbled up from below.

'Come here, Henry,' he called, waving the lead, as the dog stopped by the side of the road. Head down and tail up, he began sniffing eagerly all round the ground. 'Henry!' Joe shouted. 'Henry come here!'

At that moment, Joe spotted what

Henry had smelled. It was a small, pink warthog-like creature with floppy ears and a curly tail, standing motionless on top of a tussock surrounded by lily-pads and bubbling mud. It was staring, unblinkingly, at the dog.

'HENRY!' Joe yelled.

With a loud yelp of excitement, Henry suddenly bounded forwards and took a flying leap at the tussock. 'Oh, no! He thinks it's a squirrel,' shouted Joe, jumping off Norbert's shoulder and chasing after him.

'Come back!' shouted Randalf. 'Never chase a pink stinky hog!'

'Why not?' asked Norbert.

'In case you catch it, stupid!' said Veronica.

'Henry!' shouted Joe as, leaping from tussock to tussock, he tried to catch up. The more puffed out he became, the more difficult it was to keep his balance. 'Henry, come . . . *Aaargh!*'

SPLASH!

Joe fell face down in the purple mud. Ahead, Henry caught up with the pink stinky hog and lunged for its tail. With a high-pitched squeal, the hog raised its rump and broke wind with astonishing force. The sound—like a small cannon exploding—echoed round the Perfumed Bog. And the smell . . . !

'Someone's caught a pink stinky hog,' said Randalf.

In the Perfumed Bog, Joe picked himself up. The smell was eye-wateringly horrendous. Henry seemed to be in shock. The pink stinky hog stood on its little tussock triumphantly, tail in the air. From behind it, a small hill rose up from the purple mud.

It had two piggy pink eyes that regarded Henry and Joe unblinkingly. It had a piggy pink snout that wrinkled as it sniffed the air and let out deep piggy snorts of anger. Its two huge tusks glinted in the pink light of the

132

Perfumed Bog.

'Henry,' said Joe softly. 'Time to go, Henry.'

With a whimper, Henry backed away.

The huge pink stinky hog climbed on to the tussock beside the pink stinky hog piglet, slowly turned its back on Joe and Henry and raised its great rump high in the air.

'Henry!' shouted Joe. 'Run for it!'

A sound like a huge cannon exploding echoed round the Perfumed Bog. *And the smell . . . !*

'Someone's caught a pink stinky hog's mother,' said Randalf.

Just then, Henry shot out of the swirling pink mist and on to the path. Moments later, Joe scrambled after him.

'All aboard,' shouted Norbert, picking them both up.

'To the Ogrehills, Norbert!' shouted Randalf. 'And remember, until we get there, breathe through your mouths!'

The sun was setting as they approached the Ogrehills. Randalf's snores and the gentle thud of Norbert's footfalls were the only sounds in the still air—at least they were until they were joined by another sound, equally tuneless.

'*La, la, la . . .*'

The sound floated across the evening sky. Joe looked up, and there, marching along the road towards them from Elfwood was a stooped, shadowy figure in a cloak and raised hood. Under his arm was a roll of what looked like cloth or carpet.

The tuneless song became louder.

'*La, la, la, la-la.*'

Joe shivered, and the hairs at the back of his neck stood on end.

As the lone figure came closer he lowered his hood, and Joe was surprised to see a familiar face.

'Grubbers!' Randalf exclaimed. 'How good to see you again.'

Grubley looked up. *'Randy,'* he said. 'Out and about, eh? And I see you've got your warrior-hero with you, all kitted out for battle.'

'La, la, la . . .'

'You bet,' said Randalf. 'We're on important business for the Horned Baron, aren't we Joe?'

But Joe did not reply. He was listening to the singing.

'*La, la, la . . .*

Joe frowned. The noise seemed to be coming from the roll of material under Grubley's arm.

'Yes, we're heading for the Ogrehills,' Randalf was saying.

'Rather you than me,' said Grubley, pulling a face.

'Oh, I have absolute faith that your warrior outfit will do its job,' said Randalf.

'You get what you pay for,' said Grubley.

'Precisely,' said Randalf. 'But I am being rude. Norbert,' he said, 'help me down.'

'Oh, don't get down on my account,' said Grubley. 'I'm already running late as it is.'

'*La, la, la. La, la, la.*' The tuneless song was louder than ever. Had no one else noticed? Joe wondered.

'Running late?' said Randalf, tutting sympathetically. 'But what are you doing so far from Goblintown in the first place?'

'*La, la, la.*'

'I'm on important business for the

136

Horned Baron, too,' said Grubley, raising the frayed, faded and somewhat grubby roll of musical cloth. 'Oh, I've been given the runaround, I can tell you,' he said crossly. 'Been looking all over, I have.' He sighed. 'It's all down to that Horned Baron's wife . . .'

'Ingrid?' said Randalf.

'The Horned Baron only had one wife the last time I looked,' said Grubley. 'She wants a set of singing curtains. Never heard of them myself, but she swears blind she saw them in my catalogue. And what Ingrid wants, Ingrid gets!'

Randalf nodded knowingly.

'So, I've been traipsing around,' he said. 'Here, there and everywhere. Luckily, I've got my contacts,' he added, and tapped his nose. 'I managed to lay my hands on this. Enchanted material. Very rare, I can tell you. I'm heading back to Goblintown to have it made into singing curtains.'

'La, la, la . . .'

'Call that singing?' said Veronica. 'More like mournful mooing . . .'

'Shut up, Veronica,' said Randalf.

137

'I'm sure Ingrid will love them.'

'I hope so,' muttered Grubley, as he turned and hurried off towards Goblintown. 'I do hope so.'

The landscape grew stony and barren as they neared the Ogrehills. Scrubby bushes gave way to tufts of grass, prickleweeds and fat-leafed succulents which Norbert seemed to find irresistible.

'Yum, there's another one,' he said, and abruptly stooped down, broke off a leaf and pushed it into his mouth. Cries of alarm and distress came from his shoulders as Randalf clung on desperately, Veronica flapped about and Joe tried his best to keep Henry from slipping off his lap. 'Be-lish-ush!' he muttered slurpily.

'Norbert, will you *stop* doing that!' said Randalf sharply. 'You nearly sent us *all* flying that time!'

'Sorry, sir,' said Norbert. 'It's just, I haven't had squishweeds for ages. I'd forgotten how much I like them.'

'Yes, well, I think you've had enough now,' said Randalf. 'I know you. You see something you like and you don't know when to stop. Don't make a pink stinky hog of yourself.'

'No, sir,' said Norbert. 'Sorry, sir.'

'Now get a move on, Norbert,' said Randalf. 'There's a good fellow.'

On they went. The rolling Ogrehills stretched off into the distance.

'That ogre must be around here somewhere. Keep your eyes peeled for squeezed sheep,' said Randalf.

Joe scanned the area all around him. 'What on earth does a squeezed sheep look like, anyway?' Joe wondered out loud.

'Exactly as you'd imagine,' said Veronica.

'Hmmph, said Joe. 'Well I can't see *any* sheep, squeezed or otherwise. In fact, I can't see much of anything,' he added. 'Apart from rocks.'

'Keep looking,' Randalf said. 'You too, Veronica.'

'If you insist,' said Veronica. 'It's so horrible here. Dry, dusty, desolate. Why would anyone want to live in a place like this?'

'This is where *I* lived,' said Norbert, with a smile. 'I think it's kind of homely.'

'You're right, Norbert,' said Veronica. 'If your idea of home is a rock for a pillow and a sandpit for a bed.'

'A sandpit bed?' said Norbert. 'Pure luxury. I and my twenty brothers had to sleep on pebbles. And we'd have given anything for a rock pillow. Prickleweed, that's what we had. And if we wanted to go to the loo in the middle of the night, we had to—'

'Yes, yes, Norbert,' said Randalf. 'That'll do. Just keep looking for a sheep.'

'There's one!' Joe shouted excitedly, and pointed ahead. 'Over there! Look!'

'Are you sure it's not a rock?' said Randalf.

'It's moving,' said Joe.

'So it is,' said Randalf. 'Proceed, Norbert.'

As they approached, it was clear that it was indeed a sheep, and not a happy one at that. It was wandering around in circles, looking dazed and bewildered. Its wool was bunched up around its shoulders and hindquarters, and squeezed flat in the middle. It looked like a walking, woolly dumb-bell. When it noticed the ogre stomping resolutely towards it, it let out an odd squeaky bleat, turned on its heels and disappeared over the ridge in a cloud of dust.

'That sheep has definitely been squeezed!' said Randalf. 'After it!'

Norbert tried his best, but the terrified sheep had given them the slip. It wasn't long, however, before Veronica spotted two more.

'Over there!' she said, flapping her wing at the pair of cowering, shivering sheep with wild eyes and dumb-bell wool. 'Freshly squeezed sheep!'

'Good work, Veronica,' said Randalf. 'And if we follow their trail, it'll lead straight to the culprit—none other than Engelbert the Enormous, I'll be bound!'

Joe swallowed hard. 'I'm feeling a bit nervous,' he admitted quietly.

'Joe, Joe, Joe,' said Randalf, as if talking to a very young child. 'We aren't nervous, are we? Of course we remember we've got our Trident of Trickery. Ooh, scary trident! We've got our Helmet of Sarcasm. Nasty, nasty helmet! All we've got to do is show this Engelbert character who's boss. Who's the boss, Joe? Who's the boss?'

'I'm the boss,' said Joe uncertainly. 'I'm the boss.'

Norbert trudged on, following the sheep's trail. Up and down the undulating rockscape, he went; deeper and deeper into the Ogrehills. Occasionally, they passed the mouths of caves, from which came the sleepy sounds of snoozing ogres.

'Mummy, mummy,' growled some.

'My snuggly-wuggly,' murmured others in deep, gruff voices.

And the air was filled with the slurps of thumbs being sucked and mighty rumbling snores.

'D . . . do you think we're getting close?' Joe asked in a trembling voice.

Randalf nodded. 'Judging by that unfortunate mess over there,' he said. 'That is where our sheep were squeezed. Quiet, everyone!'

The wind abruptly dropped and the air became oddly still. Norbert put Randalf and Joe down, and Joe clipped Henry on the lead. Veronica sat on Randalf's head, feathers ruffled. They all listened intently.

'It's quiet,' she said in a hushed voice. 'Too quiet. I don't like it.'

'Shut up, Veronica,' whispered Randalf, who was thinking exactly the same thing.

'What exactly are we listening for?' whispered Joe.

Just then, an anguished bleat echoed loudly round the hills, and a sheep— with bulging eyes and squeezed wool— came hurtling over the ridge and dashed away across the stony ground.

'What the . . . ?' Randalf began.

'NO!' boomed a loud and angry voice. 'IT'S NOT THE SAME! IT'S NOT THE SAME AT ALL!'

Joe stared in horror in the direction the voice had come from, and as he stared, he heard banging and crashing and a series of loud thuds. A thick cloud of dust rose up.

'OH, WHERE IS IT?' the great voice demanded. 'WHERE, OH, WHERE HAS IT GONE?'

'D . . . do you think *th . . . that's* Engelbert?' whispered Joe.

'Unless I'm very much mistaken,' Randalf whispered back.

'He *sounds* enormous.'

'Oh, I'm sure he won't be *that* enormous,' said Randalf reassuringly. 'Come on, now, Joe the Barbarian.

144

Raise high your Trident of Trickery, adjust your Helmet of Sarcasm and let your Wellies of Power lead you to victory.'

'SOMEONE'S DEFINITELY *STOLEN* IT!' the voice raged. 'AND WHEN I FIND OUT WHO IT IS, I'LL . . . I'LL . . .'

'The time has come, Joe the Barbarian,' said Randalf, pushing Joe forwards. 'Go forth and confront him. You can do it!'

With his trident in one hand and his dog-lead in the other, Joe walked ahead on rubbery legs. Henry cowered by his side.

All at once a truly massive ogre head—more than twice the size of Norbert's—appeared above a ridge. Joe froze. The head was swiftly followed by colossal shoulders, a barrel chest, a bulging gut, legs like tree trunks and feet like boats, until an entire monstrous ogre stood before him. Joe couldn't move.

The ogre roared furiously and advanced, picking up great boulders and looking underneath them, before tossing them aside.

'WHERE ARE YOU?' he bellowed, his face purple and contorted with rage, his bloodshot eyes bulging in their sockets. 'WHERE *ARE* YOU?' The light glinted on the drool that dripped from his gnashing tusks. Then his three eyes fell on Joe. The ogre paused for what seemed to the reluctant warrior-hero an eternity.

'Oh, my goodness,' Randalf gasped. 'He does seem rather upset doesn't he?'

'I do hope Joe will be all right,' said Norbert anxiously.

Joe raised his trident bravely. 'It's all a matter of psychology,' he reminded himself. He met the ogre's fearsome gaze. 'I . . . I'm a warrior-hero, from afar,' he said. 'Joe the Barbarian! And . . . *um* . . . unless you stop all this nonsense right now I'll have to smack your bottom!'

The ogre blinked.

Joe turned to the others. 'Shall I use the Helmet of Sarcasm?' he hissed. He adjusted his helmet. 'And by the way, I'm sure no one has *ever* told you that your face looks just like the rear end of a pink stinky hog . . .'

The ogre threw back his head and the Ogrehills trembled with his mighty roar.

'What do we do now?' squeaked Joe.

'There's only one thing we can do!' said Randalf. *'RUN!'*

With their hearts in their mouths and
dust in their hair, they made a
desperate dash for it. Their panicked
cries broke the silence. Randalf ran
blindly on till he could run no more.
Stopping abruptly, he bent double and
gulped for air.

'That was close,' said Veronica,
landing daintily on the wizard's rump.

'You can say that again,' said
Norbert, stomping up behind them.

'That was clo—'

'Shut up, Veronica!' Randalf panted
impatiently. He straightened up and
shook his head. 'Most unusual,' he

said. 'I've never known an ogre that angry before. He should have been terrified of our warrior-hero here . . .'

'Where?' said Veronica.

'Here,' said Randalf. 'Joe . . . Oh, no. Where is he?'

'Joe?' cried Norbert. 'Joe, where are you? Joe! Joe!'

'For crying out loud, Randalf!' said Veronica irritably. 'First sign of trouble and you turn tail and leave him to it.'

'But he was right behind me,' said Randalf, looking all around him. 'And I distinctly gave the order to run. It's not my fault he didn't hear me. That Helmet of Sarcasm must have slipped down over his ears . . .'

'He's gone!' Norbert wailed. 'And so is Henry!'

'Typical!' said Veronica. 'It's Quentin all over again.'

'We've got to go back for them,' Norbert sobbed tearfully.

'Now, let's not be hasty,' said Randalf nervously. 'You saw the mood that ogre was in. Perhaps we should allow the dust to settle a bit first, then, in a week or so, we can . . .'

'*You* brought the lad here to the Ogrehills,' interrupted Veronica accusingly. 'You can't abandon him now. You'd never be able to live with yourself.'

Randalf examined his fingernails closely. 'Of course, I feel bad. Don't get me wrong, Veronica. We *all* do! But be realistic . . .'

'Poor Joe! Poor Henry!' Norbert wailed. And poor, dear Quentin. *Boo-hoo!*'

'"Trust me, I'm a wizard", that's what you said,' Veronica continued. 'And he *did* trust you. Joe the Barbarian trusted *you*. And now, how are you repaying that trust? Eh? By abandoning him.' She clacked her beak reproachfully. 'You're a disgrace! If we don't go back right now, then I'm leaving you!'

'Please sir, please,' said Norbert, sobbing even louder. 'If we could just go and check. Maybe there's a chance . . .'

Randalf sighed. 'All right, all right,' he said. 'You win! I'm just too soft-hearted, that's my trouble! A fool to myself sometimes. Come, let's get this

150

over with. Follow me. He turned and gathered up his robes. 'But keep close.'

Huddled together for safety, Randalf and Norbert retraced their footsteps, creeping back silently, with Veronica keeping a watchful look out from the top of Randalf's head.

'I think we're getting close,' she announced after a while and flapped her wing up ahead. 'Look at those giant footprints, and how the dust has all been stirred up.'

Randalf nodded. Norbert began whimpering.

'Sssssh!' hissed Randalf, placing a finger to his lips. 'We don't want to . . .'

'*OH, NO!*' wailed Norbert, and pointed at a bent piece of three-pronged metal. '*LOOK!*'

It was the Trident of Trickery, twisted out of shape and lying discarded in the dust. Randalf picked it up and shuddered.

'And there!' Veronica cried. She flew down and landed on an abandoned Welly of Power.

Norbert howled with grief. 'Oh, Joe,' he blubbed. He picked up the lone rubber boot and hugged it desperately. 'It must have come off,' he sobbed, 'when he . . . when he . . . he . . .' He straightened up and scanned the horizon for any sign of his latest warrior-hero friend. Apart from one set of massive footprints in the dust which marched up and over the ridge, there was nothing. 'JOE!' he cried. *JOE!'*

The desperate sound echoed round the barren hills and faded away unanswered.

JOE!'
Veronica flapped up and landed on his shoulder. 'I don't think Joe can hear you,' she said softly.

'You never know,' said Norbert, his pleading voice willing it to be true. 'If there's one thing my great-uncle Larry the Unlucky taught me it was that you should never give up hope. "Something will turn up." That's what he used to say, before the dragon ate him. "Something will turn up . . ."'

'I'm afraid *this* has turned up,' said Randalf gently. He held out a flattened disc of dull silver.

'Wh . . . what's that?' Norbert trembled.

Randalf showed him the bent black handle sticking out from one side. 'The Helmet of Sarcasm,' he said.

'No,' Norbert gasped. 'It can't be . . . You don't mean . . .'

'As you so rightly said,' Veronica muttered bitterly to Randalf, 'you get what you pay for.' She tutted. 'Skinflint!'

'But it *can't* be his helmet,' said Norbert, fingering the flat piece of metal. 'Please say it isn't.'

'I'm afraid it is,' said Randalf. He shook his head. 'Completely flattened. Pulverized. Spifflicated. Flatter than a burst gas frog, you might even say . . .'

'Stop it!' Norbert howled, and clamped his hands over his ears. 'Stop it! Stop it! Stop it!'

'There, there,' said Randalf, and patted Norbert on the arm. 'It's all right, Norbert.'

'But it's *not* all right, sir!' Norbert bawled. 'It's not all right at all. First Quentin. Now Joe!' He pulled a grubby hankie from his pocket and blew his nose loudly. 'I just can't bear it!'

Veronica rounded on Randalf. 'You're to blame for all this!' she squawked. 'I never thought Joe was up to it. Warrior-hero, indeed!'

'But he *was*,' Randalf protested. 'I summoned him myself

'You summoned *Quentin!*' said Veronica. 'And look at him!'

'*Oh-woh-woh!*' wailed Norbert.

'Norbert, calm yourself,' said Randalf. 'We can summon more warrior-heroes. Even better ones . . .'

'*OH-OH-WOH!*'

'Third time lucky, eh?' said Veronica. 'My goodness, Randalf, you can be unfeeling at times. Why don't you bring the twisted toasting fork and squashed saucepan with you?' she suggested scornfully. 'Maybe you can get a refund!'

'Now, there's an idea,' said Randalf thoughtfully.

'OH-WOH-WOH!'

'A *bad* idea,' Randalf added hastily 'Of course, I wouldn't dream of . . .'

'You're right,' said Veronica. 'Grubley would never agree to it.'

'Veronica!' said Randalf sharply. 'I'm surprised at you. Don't take any notice of her, Norbert.'

'So, what *are* we going to do, sir?' Norbert asked tearfully.

'Well, we can't stay here,' said Randalf. 'And I don't fancy going back to the Horned Baron. If we tell him that the rogue ogre is still at large — and that we've lost our warrior-hero into the bargain,' he continued as Norbert sniffled into his hanky, 'he won't be a happy Horned Baron.'

'I'm not happy,' said the Horned Baron, pacing up and down the great reception hall. 'I'm not happy at all!' He was working himself up into a right state.

For a start, Ingrid had been on at him all day about her precious singing curtains—and he hadn't heard a word from Grubley ever since he'd handed over the pouchful of silver pipsqueaks. Worse still, the castle had been plagued by a constant stream of goblins, elves and trolls all complaining that their crops had been flattened, their thatched-roofs torn off, their sheep squeezed—and what was he, as Horned Baron of Muddle Earth, going to do about it? That's what they all wanted to know.

'It's all in hand,' he'd kept telling them. 'Even now, a famous wizard and a highly trained warrior-hero are on their way to deal with the rogue ogre.' Yet, even to himself, the words hadn't quite rung true.

The Horned Baron grunted. 'Randalf the *Wise*, indeed! I've worn wiser pairs of underpants!'

He glanced at the clock for the tenth time in as many minutes and strode over to the window.

'All this intolerable waiting!' he groaned as he stared out. 'That's the trouble with being so powerful and important. You spend half your life waiting for others to carry out your commands!'

'WAL-TER!'

Ingrid's strident voice cut through the air like a rusty knife, sending the dust flying and setting the Horned Baron's teeth on edge. He closed his eyes and slowly counted to ten. For a moment there, he'd quite forgotten about his wife. This was never a sensible thing to do.

'WALTER!' she screeched. The crystal chandelier tinkled softly. 'Can you hear me?'

'Nine . . . ten.' The Horned Baron opened his eyes. 'Loud and clear, my little snuggle-muffin,' he called back.

'Don't you "snuggle-muffin" me,' Ingrid shouted. 'Where are my singing curtains? That's what I want to know. Where *are* they, Walter?'

'Everything's in hand,' the Horned Baron replied. 'I'm expecting them at any moment.'

'That's what you said an hour ago,' Ingrid countered. 'But every time there's a knock on the door, it's someone else complaining about their wretched sheep!'

'Any moment now,' the Horned Baron assured her.

'You'd better not be lying to me, Walter,' said Ingrid, her voice becoming more threatening as it grew quieter. 'You remember what happened last time I caught you lying, don't you?'

'All too well,' the Horned Baron called back, and smoothed his straggly moustache tenderly. The green dye had almost grown out.

'Next time, I'll use the whole bottle!' she shouted.

The Horned Baron winced and looked out miserably at the empty road. 'Where are you, Grubley?' he muttered. 'Don't let me down . . .'

'*And* a wire brush!' Ingrid added.

The Horned Baron's eyes grew

steely. 'If you do let me down, Grubley, there'll be a place waiting for you beside Randalf down in the dungeons.'

'Walter!'

'The smallest dungeon with no window.'

'Walter!'

'And twenty hand-picked stinky hogs for company . . .'

'There's someone at the door, Walter!' Ingrid shrieked. 'Do I have to do *everything* myself?'

'And regular visits from the Baroness,' muttered the Horned Baron, trotting towards the door. 'I'm on my way, my sweet!'

'Well done!' shouted Ingrid sarcastically. 'And for your sake, Walter, I hope it's those singing curtains turned up at last. I'm sick to death of hearing about squeezed sheep. I want to be lulled, Walter. I want to be soothed . . .'

'And so you shall, my honeyed sugarplum,' the Horned Baron called back.

He opened the door. A short, slight individual with a striped tunic and a feather in his cap stood on the top step. 'Greetings-elf!' he announced. 'I bring greetings from Mr Grubley of Goblintown.'

'Is there a package to go with the greetings?' the Horned Baron asked hopefully.

'No, just a message,' said the elf, lowering his head and shaking it regretfully.

The Horned Baron rolled his eyes. 'So, what is the message?' he asked.

The elf took a deep breath and cleared his throat. 'Having travelled to the four corners of Muddle Earth, Grubley of Goblintown has procured a length of enchanted material which, even now, is being transformed into singing curtains, the like of which have never before been seen or heard.'

'Thank goodness for that,' the Horned Baron muttered.

'However . . .' the elf continued.

The Horned Baron raised his hand. *'However?'* he said. 'I don't like the sound of that.'

'I could skip to the "best wishes" if you like,' said the elf.

'Is there nothing about when the curtains will be ready?' asked the Horned Baron.

'That's part of the "however",' said the elf.

The Horned Baron tutted. Above his head, he could hear Ingrid stomping backwards and forwards with growing impatience. 'All right, then,' he sighed. 'Get on with it.'

'However,' the elf resumed, 'due to unforeseen circumstances, the curtains are taking somewhat longer to make than expected. They will be delivered to you tomorrow teatime at the very latest, probably . . .'

'Tomorrow teatime!' gasped the Horned Baron. *'Probably!'*

'*Grubley's Discount Store* would like to take this opportunity to apologize for any inconvenience . . .'

The Horned Baron snorted. 'You don't know the half of it,' he muttered. 'I don't know how I'm going to explain all this to her upstairs.' He shook his head. 'Is that it, then?' he asked the greetings-elf.

The elf nodded. 'Just about,' he said.

He held out his hand. 'That'll be three brass muckles.'

'What?' said the Horned Baron. 'You mean Grubley sent a greetings-elf without paying for the stamp?'

'Ah, yes,' said the elf. 'I forgot. There's a PS. Sorry about the stamp. It can come off my final bill when we settle up.'

'Final bill!' the Horned Baron shouted. 'Settle up! I'll settle up all right. One dungeon, twenty pink stinky hogs and a no-good wizard should just about do it!'

'Is that the message you wish to send back?' asked the greetings-elf.

'Yes, I . . .' The Horned Baron frowned and stroked his chin. 'That is, *no*,' he said.

'No?'

'No,' the Horned Baron confirmed. 'Simply thank Grubley for his message and tell him I look forward to his arrival . . .'

'WALTER!'

'His *speedy* arrival,' he corrected himself.

'OK,' said the greetings-elf, 'though

personally, I liked the stinky hogs message better myself.' He stuck out his open palm a second time.

The Horned Baron sighed and dropped three muckles into the outstretched hand. The greetings-elf pulled a stamp from a pocket, licked it and stuck it on his forehead. Then he turned and skipped off down the stairs and away. For a fleeting instant, the Horned Baron imagined that *he* was a greetings-elf, setting off without a care in the world.

'*WAL*-TER!!'

The carefree daydream popped. He closed the door. 'Yes, my sweetness,' he called up the stairs.

'Was that my curtains?' she shouted back.

'Not as such,' the Horned Baron confessed.

163

'What's that supposed to mean?' demanded Ingrid.

'It was *news of* your curtains, my sweet,' he explained. 'There has been a slight hitch . . .'

'*Hitch,* Walter?' said Ingrid. 'I don't like the word *hitch.* You know that. I don't like it at all.'

'I know, my turtle dove,' said the Horned Baron soothingly. 'There have been unforeseen circumstances. You know how it is! Grubley's promised me they'll be here tomorrow,' he added.

'*Tomorrow!*' screeched Ingrid. 'But what am I supposed to do tonight? I shan't be able to sleep a wink, I just know I shan't. And you know what I can be like when I'm over-tired.'

'Indeed, I do,' said the Horned Baron wearily.

'Grumpy, Walter. I shall be very grumpy. You won't recognize me!

'Oh, I think I might,' he muttered beneath his breath. 'Believe me, Ingrid,' he called upstairs, 'you just can't rush these things. I mean, singing curtains, Ingrid, fashioned from only the finest enchanted cloth, tasselled

164

and sequinned, and hand-stitched by a master sewing-elf. It'll be well worth the wait when they do arrive, you have my word . . .'

'*If* they arrive,' Ingrid shouted, and the entire castle shook as she slammed the door of her bedchamber hard shut. The sound of loud thuds and muffled sobs echoed above as Ingrid threw herself around the room.

The Horned Baron shook his head. 'This is all your fault, Grubley,' he said. 'I mean, why put a blasted advertisement for blasted singing curtains in that blasted catalogue of yours if you don't actually have any blasted singing curtains in stock and have to go chasing round Muddle Earth searching for some? Blasted funny way to run a business!' His eyes narrowed. 'You've upset my beloved Ingrid, that's what you've done—and when Ingrid's upset, *I'm* upset! And when I'm upset . . .'

'The Horned Baron's going to be so pleased with me,' said Grubley.

'So you already said,' the goblin muttered as he rethreaded his sewing-elf. 'Twice.'

'But he is!' said Grubley. 'I can't wait to see his face . . .'

'*La, la, la,*' sang the material.

The goblin picked up a large, shiny pair of scissors, laid the material out across the workbench and began to cut it in half.

'*La, la . . . Ouch! Ouch! Ouch!*'

'Will you stop doing that!' shouted the goblin, and slammed the scissors down. He turned to Grubley. 'You see the trouble I'm having! Every time I try and cut the cloth in two, it makes a racket. And it's *very* off-putting,' he said. 'Are you absolutely sure you want curtains? I could do you a very nice roller blind.'

Grubley shook his head. 'Apparently, the catalogue specified singing *curtains*,' he said, 'and the Horned Baroness has set her heart on them.'

The goblin picked up the scissors again. 'I don't know why you advertised something you don't keep in stock in the first place,' he grumbled.

'That's the strangest thing,' said Grubley. 'I don't remember putting them in the catalogue.'

'Well, someone must have,' said the goblin.

'I know,' said Grubley, frowning. 'I just don't understand it.' He looked up. 'Still, I've got the cloth now. That's the most important thing. And as soon as you've made it up as curtains, I'll get them over to the Horned Baron's castle. So if you wouldn't mind . . .'

'It's all right for you,' said the goblin. 'You don't have to work with material that won't keep quiet.' He fingered the frayed cloth, which gave a high-pitched squeak. 'Giving me the heebie-jeebies, it is.'

'Here, said Grubley, reaching into his pocket and pulling out a pair of large furry earmuffs. 'Try these.'

The goblin stared at them. 'What am I supposed to do with them?' he said.

'They're earmuffs, stupid,' said Grubley irritably. 'You put them over your ears.'

167

The goblin did as he was told, flattened out the material and raised his thumbs. He hadn't heard a thing.

'Excellent,' said Grubley. 'Now get on with the curtains.

The goblin looked at him blankly.

'*Get on with the curtains!*' shouted Grubley.

The goblin frowned and mouthed the word, *what?*

Irritated, Grubley lifted one of the earmuffs and leaned forwards. 'GET ON WITH THE CURTAINS!' he bellowed into the goblin's ear.

'All right, all right,' the goblin said, pushing the earmuffs back into place. 'I'm not deaf!'

'Give me strength!' Grubley muttered.

The goblin sat down on the stool, picked up his scissors again and this time—despite the singing, wailing and frequent cries of *'Ouch!'*—cut the cloth and set the sewing-elf off stitching at a furious pace.

'Very nice,' said Grubley, holding the curtains up at last. 'Very homely. A genuine pair of singing curtains.'

'*La, la, la. La, la, la,*' sang the

curtains, in a discordant duet.

'Call that singing!' said the goblin. 'More like . . .'

'Oh, don't you start,' said Grubley. 'The Horned Baroness is tone deaf. She'll love them, and that's all that matters.' He frowned. 'Randalf the Wise,' he said. *'Wise,* indeed! Heading for the Ogrehills, he was. Not very wise at all, if you ask me!'

'We came, we saw, we ran away,' said Veronica from the top of Randalf's head as Norbert trudged back down the mountain road. 'Joe the Barbarian, mighty warrior-hero and Henry the Hairy, faithful battle-hound—missing, presumed pulverized . . .'

'Yes, all right, Veronica,' said Randalf. 'You've made your point.'

'Engelbert the Enormous,' she continued, 'missing, presumed sheep squeezing . . .'

'Shut *up*, Veronica!' said Randalf.

Norbert wiped away a tear. 'Have you decided where we're going yet, sir?' he asked.

Randalf sighed and nodded. 'Home,' he said.

'Home, sir?' said Norbert.

'Yes, Norbert,' said Randalf. 'Let's go home.'

Two of Muddle Earth's three moons were high in the sky. They shone down brightly on a gathering of twenty or so ogres who were all sitting in front of their caves, around a huge, roaring fire. The air echoed with the sound of soft, satisfied slurping as the ogres sucked their thumbs.

One ogre—the biggest of them all—was rubbing a dog slowly up and down his cheek, and smiling happily. The dog was wagging his tail and emitting a curious yodelling bark of utter contentment.

One of the ogres removed his thumb

from his mouth and turned to the boy
next to him. 'Old Engelbert's just his
old self again,' he said.

'Yeah, you *have* calmed him down,
Joe,' said another.

'He just needed a bit of
understanding,' said the first ogre.

'It's all any of us need,' chipped in a
third.

'After all,' said the first, 'how would
you like it if you'd lost your special

snuggly-wuggly?' He held up a tatty teddy with one eye, one ear, one arm and no legs. 'I don't know what I'd do if Trumpet ever went missing!'

Joe nodded. He couldn't quite believe what he was seeing or hearing. The other ogres held up their own snuggly-wugglies one after the other— a grubby fluffy bunny, a fuzzy blanket, a tattered scrap of towel . . .

'Course, Engelbert was always particularly proud of his snuggly-wuggly,' said the first ogre. 'Bit niffy, it was. And threadbare. But Engelbert loved it. And do you know why?'

'Why?' said Joe.

' 'Cause it was enchanted,' said the ogre. 'It sang.'

'Did it now?' said Joe thoughtfully.

'His mother got it for him when he was a baby,' the ogre went on. 'From one of the wizards on the Enchanted Lake. Roger the Wrinkled, his name was . . .'

'Course, that was back before the wizards disappeared,' the second ogre interrupted. 'You can't get anything enchanted these days. That snuggly-wuggly was unique. Irreplaceable.'

'Which is why Engelbert took it so badly when it went missing. It used to lull him to sleep every night.'

'Engelbert loved his snuggly-wuggly,' said the second ogre. 'He said it smelled of warm hugs. Took it everywhere, he did . . .'

Engelbert, *who* had clearly been listening in, suddenly sat forwards. 'Until somebody took it!' he exclaimed. 'I woke up last week and there it was, gone.' His face clouded over. 'Stolen, it was! Someone had stolen my snuggly-wuggly. My lovely singing snuggly-wuggly . . .'

'Steady on, big fellow,' the other ogres told him. 'Stay calm.'

'It made Engelbert angry,' Engelbert continued, his voice trembling and his face all blotchy and red. 'And sheep are no good: They might be soft, but they make such *a horrible* sound—even when you hardly squeeze them at all.'

Henry barked excitedly, and licked Engelbert's bulbous nose. A broad smile spread over the ogre's features.

'Not like Henry here,' he said. 'He

has a lovely singing voice.'

'This snuggly-wuggly,' said Joe. 'Did it go *la, la, la* . . . ?' he crooned, singing in his deepest, groaniest voice.

'Yes,' said the ogres excitedly. 'How did you know?'

'I think I may have seen it,' he said, as he remembered his encounter with Grubley on the road from Elfwood.

Anyway, it doesn't matter now,' Engelbert said. 'I don't need my old snuggly-wuggly back. Not now I've got Henry.' He rubbed him affectionately up and down his cheek again.

Henry wagged his tail with pleasure and barked his strange yodelling bark. Engelbert chuckled.

'Just listen to that,' he said, and tickled him under his tummy. 'He's perfect.'

Joe nodded sadly. '*I* think so,' he said. 'The thing is, Engelbert, he belongs to me. And I would miss him, too. I've had him ever since he was a little puppy.'

Engelbert looked up. His jaw dropped. 'You're . . . you're not going to take him away, are you?' he said.

'You wouldn't leave Engelbert without a snuggly-wuggly again? I couldn't bear it.'

'And you know what happened last time,' the other ogres warned him.

'I know,' said Joe. He turned to Engelbert. 'But, supposing I could get your real snuggly-wuggly back,' he said. 'You'd let me have Henry back then, wouldn't you?'

The ogre pouted. 'I don't know about that,' he said reluctantly.

'Engelbert, I'm talking about your *old* snuggly-wuggly,' said Joe softly. 'Your *best* snuggly-wuggly. The snuggly-wuggly you've had since you were a baby ogre, that sings you to sleep and smells of warm hugs.' He smiled. 'The snuggly-wuggly you love as much as I love Henry.'

Engelbert looked at Joe, then at Henry—then back at Joe.

'All right, then,' he said at last. 'It's a deal.'

Shortly after teatime the following day there was a loud knock at the castle door. The Horned Baron ran to answer it. Grubley was standing there.

'At last!' the Horned Baron exclaimed. 'You took for ever!'

'Singing curtains can't be rushed,' Grubley explained. Having passed the greetings-elf halfway between Goblintown and the castle, he already knew how desperate the Horned Baron was to receive them. 'Besides,' he added, 'what's all this stuff about dungeons and wizards and pink stinky hogs?'

'Never mind!' the Horned Baron humphed. 'You've got them, that's the important thing.' He frowned. 'Where are they?'

Grubley took off his backpack and opened it up. The sound of two muffled voices singing in discordant harmony filled the hallway. Grubley pulled out the pair of curtains and displayed them over a crooked elbow.

'They look a bit tatty,' said the Horned Baron. He wrinkled his nose. 'And they niff a bit,' he added. 'Perhaps you'd see your way to knocking a little bit off the final price . . .'

'You must be joking,' said Grubley, outraged. 'These singing curtains are unique. You wouldn't believe the lengths I had to go to to find them.'

The droning song grew louder. It echoed round the vaulted ceiling and floated up the stairs.

'Walter!' came a strident, yet hopeful, voice. 'Is that *singing* I can hear? Have my singing curtains finally arrived?'

'Y . . . yes, they have,' the Horned Baron called up. 'If you can call that tuneless cacophony *singing*,' he muttered under his breath.

'Course, you don't have to have them,' said Grubley, folding the curtains up. 'If you don't want them, I know plenty who do . . .'

'Oh, Walter,' Ingrid replied. 'You wonderful Horned Baron, you! I knew you wouldn't let me down. I never doubted you for a moment.'

'But if you *do* want them,' Grubley continued, as he opened his backpack, 'then, as you well know, you owe me a pouch of silver pipsqueaks.'

'Daylight robbery,' the Horned Baron complained. 'One pouch is more than enough . . .'

'WALTER!' Ingrid shrieked. 'I am a patient woman. But you are trying that patience, Walter. You are pushing it to the very limit.' She paused. 'I WANT MY SINGING CURTAINS NOW!'

'Right away,' the Horned Baron said. He turned to Grubley and thrust the pouch of silver pipsqueaks into his hand. 'I take it hanging the curtains up is included in the fee.'

'Not normally,' said Grubley. The Horned Baron's eyebrows drew together menacingly. 'But for such a valued customer,' he added in an oily voice, 'I'd be only too happy to oblige.'

Just then, there was a furious hammering at the door. Grubley jumped. The Horned Baron spun round.

'What now?' he said.

'WALTER!'

'Coming . . . I mean, going . . .' the Horned Baron called back, as he headed first for the staircase, then back for the door, not knowing for a moment whether he was coming or going.

The hammering resumed, louder than ever, and accompanied by a loud voice shouting, 'Open up! Open up! It's a matter of life and death!'

The Horned Baron raised his eyebrows to the ceiling. 'If it isn't one thing, it's another!' he said.

'WAL-TER!!'

'You take the curtains up,' the Horned Baron told Grubley. 'I'll see who's at the door. It's probably another case of badly squeezed sheep.' He shook his head. 'When I get my hands on that Randalf character . . .'

As Grubley disappeared upstairs, the Horned Baron crossed the hallway. Before he arrived at the door, however, it burst open and slammed back against the wall behind. Silhouetted in the doorway, the Horned Baron saw a wiry, dishevelled youth with matted hair, dusty clothes and one wellington boot.

'Don't tell me,' he said. 'You're here to complain that your sheep have been squeezed. Look, for the hundred-and-first time . . .'

'Horned Baron,' said Joe, as he strode into the hallway. 'Just the person I wanted to see.' He held out his hand. 'It's Joe. Remember? Joe the Barbarian? Warrior-hero?'

'Barbarian? Warrior-hero?' said the Horned Baron distractedly as he glanced past Joe and up the stairs. 'Joe . . . Ah, yes. I didn't recognize you without the saucepan on your head. How are you and how did you get on? And where's that wizard?'

From upstairs, there came the enthusiastic sound of *oohing* and *aahing*. 'Oh, Walter, they're divine!' Ingrid called. 'No one else has got anything like them. Wonderful! The very height of fashion!' There was a pause. 'They *are* the very height of fashion, aren't they, Walter?'

'Yes, dear,' he replied wearily. 'And the pinnacle of good taste.'

Joe smiled.

'New curtains,' the Horned Baron explained.

'*La, la, la. La, la, la . . .*'

'*Singing* curtains,' he explained. 'Ingrid's set her heart on them. Apparently, they're all the rage.'

'Yes,' said Joe. 'That's what Grubley said, when I saw him.'

'Singing curtains!' Ingrid trilled. 'My very own singing curtains!'

'Very rare,' said Joe. 'Very hard to come by—you don't find enchanted material every day . . .'

'And what if they are?' said the Horned Baron, suddenly defensive. 'I dare say a Horned Baron's entitled to buy his beloved wife a little gift now and then. More to the point, what are *you* doing here?'

Joe breathed in and pulled himself up to his full height. This was the part he'd been practising. 'I, Joe the Barbarian, have performed the task you bade me carry out.'

'You, what?' said the Horned Baron.

'I have brought you the head of Engelbert the Enormous.'

The Horned Baron's jaw dropped. 'You have?' he said, then frowned suspiciously. 'Where is it, then?'

'*WAAAARGH!!*'

The screeching shriek of terror was quite the loudest noise Ingrid had emitted all day. It was deafening. It made the windows rattle and the staircase shake.

'*WAAAAAARGGHH!!*'

Even the Horned Baron, who was used to Ingrid's hysterical response to spiders, bugs and not getting her own way, realized that this time, something was definitely not right. The poor woman sounded terrified out of her wits. *Something* was up there and, for the first time since Joe had burst in, the Horned Baron was pleased to have a warrior-hero in the castle.

'Follow me,' he said, turning and heading up the stairs.

As they burst into Ingrid's bedchamber, the door to her *en-suite* bathroom slammed shut.

'Get rid of it!' shrieked Ingrid from behind the door. 'It's hideous!'

The Horned Baron looked round to

see the great, knobbly, three-eyed head of Engelbert the Enormous sticking in through the window. 'What's the meaning of this?' he demanded.

'The head of Engelbert the Enormous,' said Joe. 'As you requested.'

'But it's still attached to his body!' thundered the Horned Baron. 'This is an outrage! What kind of a warrior-hero are you?'

'And what kind of a Horned Baron are *you?*' Joe retorted. 'Stooping so low as to buy curtains made out of an ogre's snuggly-wuggly!'

'An ogre's snuggly-wuggly?' said the Horned Baron with surprise.

'*La, la, la* . . .' sang one curtain tunelessly.

'*La, la, la* . . .' its neighbour droned back.

The Horned Baron's eyes widened. 'Are you telling me that these singing curtains have been fashioned from an ogre's snuggly-wuggly?'

Joe nodded. At that moment, a huge hairy hand thrust its way through the window and seized first one, then the other curtain, and whisked them away.

'Grubley!' roared the Horned Baron. 'Grubley, I demand my money back.'

But Grubley was not there. As his name echoed round the castle walls, Grubley was already on the road and hurrying back to Goblintown as fast as his legs would take him.

'One snuggly-wuggly,' Engelbert was saying as he rubbed it up and down his left cheek. 'Another snuggly-wuggly.'

He rubbed the second one up and down his right cheek. 'It's even better than before.'

'Twice as good,' said Joe, relieved that the ogre didn't seem to be upset that his snuggly-wuggly had been cut in two. 'But remember what you promised, Engelbert,' he said. 'It's time for you to keep your side of the bargain.'

'What do you mean?' said Engelbert, then winked (with his middle eye) just to show that he was joking. 'Here we are then, Joe the Barbarian,' he said and, reaching into the bed chamber again, placed Henry gently down on the rug. 'Look after him,' said Engelbert. 'He's one in a million!'

'I know he is,' said Joe, as Henry raced across the room and jumped up at him, tongue lolling and tail wagging. He looked up at the window to see Engelbert smiling back at him. 'Goodbye, Engelbert,' he said. 'And thank you.'

'Goodbye, Joe,' boomed the ogre as he stomped away. 'Goodbye, Henry,' his voice floated back.

Henry barked.

'Walter!' screeched Ingrid from the bathroom. 'That lumpy great ogre is stealing my singing curtains! Walter!'

'*La, la, la . . . La, la, la . . .*' sang the curtains—softer and softer as they were carried off, until the sound of their tuneless discord faded away completely.

'There,' said Joe to the Horned Baron. 'He's gone. And now he's got his snuggly-wuggly back, there won't be any more sheep squeezing. I can guarantee it.' He smiled. 'And now to the matter of my fee.'

'What?' exclaimed the Horned Baron.

Henry growled. The Horned Baron eyed him warily.

'Ah yes, your fee,' he said. 'A handful of brass muckles, wasn't it?'

'A pouch of silver pipsqueaks,' said Joe. 'That was what we agreed.'

'I most certainly . . .'

Henry growled again, not loudly, but just enough to remind the Horned Baron he was still there.

'. . . did,' the Horned Baron said. 'A

pouch of silver pipsqueaks it is.' He reached into the folds of his jerkin, pulled out a jangling leather pouch and, with a long, miserable sigh, reluctantly handed it over.

'Thank you,' said Joe. 'And now, if you'll excuse me, I've got to see a wizard about a journey home.'

He turned, whistled for Henry and strode back to the entrance to the bedchamber. As he reached the door, Ingrid let out a tremendous screech of rage, followed by an even louder, 'WALTER!'

The Horned Baron blanched. 'I'll see you out,' he said, as he trotted after Joe.

'WALTER!'

'That is, if I can't tempt you to stay,' he said. 'How would you like to be my personal bodyguard?'

'Errm . . . No thanks,' said Joe. He quickened his pace, taking the stairs two at a time and hurrying across the hallway. Henry kept close to heel.

'Wait a moment,' puffed the Horned Baron. 'I'll make you an offer you can't refuse . . .'

'By-eee!' Joe called back. He slammed the door shut and dashed off.

Behind him, Ingrid's voice rang out. 'Call yourself a Horned Baron!' she shrieked. 'You're pathetic! A disgrace! I'm opening the cupboard, Walter. I'm getting the green dye out, Walter—*and* the wire brush . . .'

Joe smiled to himself. What with Engelbert getting his snuggly-wuggly back and the Horned Baron getting his comeuppance, things were going rather well. Now, all he had to do was persuade Randalf to send him back home, and then *everything* would have reached a satisfactory ending.

And as for the story he had to get done when he arrived back, after his time in Muddle Earth, 'My Amazing Adventure,' would be the easiest essay he had ever had to write.

'Come on, Henry,' he said. 'Let's see if we can't make it back to the Enchanted Lake before daybreak.'

The sun had already risen by the time Joe and Henry arrived at the Enchanted Lake. As the low, bright rays of light cut through the early-morning mist, a broad, shimmering fish flopped down through the air and into the gaping beak of a waiting lazybird.

'Another day in Muddle Earth,' Joe murmured and shook his head. 'I'm almost getting used to it.' He turned to Henry. 'Almost,' he said, staring up at the great lake of water hovering high above his head. 'How on earth do we get up there?'

Henry barked and wagged his tail.

190

'Clever boy,' said Joe, for there, beside Henry, was a small bird-box on top of a pole, with a bell hanging from it on a hook. A notice said, *Ring for attention.* Joe rang the bell.

A lazybird flew out of the box, a small elf clinging to its back, and flapped upwards.

'*Ding-dong,*' droned the elf, disappearing over the lip of the lake. '*Ding-dong. Ding-dong . . .*'

Joe and Henry waited, and waited. Then a loud voice came from above. 'Grab on to the rope!'

Joe scrambled to his feet and looked up. 'Norbert!' he exclaimed.

The ogre was far up above his head and leaning precariously over the side of the water's edge. A long rope, with a basket secured to its end, was dangling down from his great fists. Joe reached out and grabbed a hold.

'That's it!' came Norbert's voice, encouragingly. 'Now climb in, both of you, and I'll pull you up.'

Trembling with unease, Joe climbed into the basket, sat cross-legged and pulled Henry on to his lap. He wound the lead around his arm, and gripped the sides of the basket tightly with both hands.

'Ready?' shouted Norbert.

'Yes,' Joe shouted back. 'As ready as I'll ever b—*Whooah!*' he cried out, as the rope jerked, the bowl wobbled and he found himself rising up, up, up into the air. He'd forgotten just how high the Enchanted Lake was.

'This is terrifying!' he shouted.

'Be thankful you're not getting up here the way the others had to,' Veronica's voice floated back. 'It took several flocks of lazybirds to lift Norbert off the ground—and you should have seen the state of his shirt when they'd finished!'

Henry whimpered. Joe hugged him and whispered that everything was going to be all right.

With a last grunt of effort, Norbert

192

pulled the basket up over the edge of the lake and held it next to a small flotilla of kitchen sinks.

Randalf and V e r o n i c a were in one, Norbert was squashed into the second, while the third was empty. All three were roped together.

Randalf leaned forwards. 'Joe!' he said.

'Randalf!' Joe replied.

'Am I glad to see you,' said Randalf.

'Not half as glad as I am to see you,' said Joe.

'Indeed, I am *twice* as glad,' Randalf insisted.

'Whatever,' said Veronica. 'Let's just get back to the houseboat before someone—mentioning no names, of course.' she said, eyeing Norbert accusingly. 'Before *someone* pulls out another plug.'

'I didn't *mean* to,' Norbert protested.

'Never mind all that, Norbert,' said Randalf. 'You're getting the basket wet. Joe, you and Henry climb into that spare kitchen sink, and Norbert will paddle us all back. Won't you, Norbert? There's a good fellow.'

Everyone took their places. Norbert began paddling furiously.

'And then you must tell me everything that happened,' Randalf shouted across the foamy water. 'Every single detail.'

'He did *what*?' Randalf exclaimed.

'He tickled Henry's tummy,' Joe repeated. 'And I could tell at once that Henry liked it. I looked round for you lot, but you'd all run off.'

Randalf coughed with embarrassment and turned a florid shade of pink. 'A tactical retreat, my lad,' he said.

'Withdrawing. Regrouping . . .'

'Running for dear life,' added Veronica.

'Shut up, Veronica,' said Randalf. 'Go on, Joe.'

'It was just like you said,' said Joe, and tapped the side of his head. 'Psychology!'

'You see,' said Randalf triumphantly. 'Didn't I tell you? With your Trident of Trickery and Helmet of Sarcasm . . .'

'Oh, no,' Joe interrupted. 'It had nothing to do with *them*. In fact, they just got in the way, so I took them off.' He looked up guiltily. 'I'm afraid they got a bit squashed when Engelbert accidentally trod on them.'

'Never mind that now,' said Randalf. 'What exactly did you mean by psychology?'

'Well, it was clear that Engelbert liked Henry,' Joe explained. 'From the moment he picked him up and rubbed him up and down his cheek, he was a changed ogre. A real softy . . .'

Randalf frowned. 'He'd lost his snuggly-wuggly, hadn't he?' he said. 'That's what he was so angry about.

And when he found Henry he calmed down again.'

Joe nodded.

'It's all falling into place,' said Randalf. 'The fits of rage. The squeezed sheep. Norbert, you should have realized.'

'Sorry, sir,' said Norbert.

'Yet Henry is with you now,' said Randalf eyeing the dog thoughtfully. 'How did you manage *to* get the ogre to give him back?'

'Simple,' said Joe. 'I found the snuggly-wuggly he'd lost.'

'Where?' asked Randalf, intrigued.

'At the Horned Baron's castle,' said Joe, and smiled at Randalf's obvious confusion. 'I'll give you a clue,' he said. 'We all saw the ogre's snuggly-wuggly earlier on,' he said, 'when we were heading for the Ogrehills. Saw it, *and* heard it . . .'

'Grubbers!' Randalf exclaimed. 'Why, he had a roll of singing material under his arm, didn't he? I remember now, he was on his way to Goblintown to have it turned into curtains for the Horned Baron's wife.' He frowned.

'Norbert, you're an ogre. I would have expected you to recognize another ogre's snuggly-wuggly.'

'Sorry, sir,' said Norbert once again. 'I don't seem to have had a very good day, do I?' he added sadly.

'Grubley, Grubley,' said Randalf, sucking air through his teeth and shaking his head. 'I never trusted him. What a rogue! What a scoundrel. Stealing an ogre's snuggly-wuggly! Because of him, the whole of Muddle Earth was thrown into turmoil.' He clapped Joe on the shoulders. 'And so it would have remained, my lad, if you hadn't come along.'

'It . . . it was nothing,' said Joe.

'Nothing?' Randalf cried. 'Why, Joe the Barbarian, warrior-hero from afar, Muddle Earth will be for ever in your debt.'

'That's great,' said Joe, 'and now, if it's all the same with you, I really *really* would like to be getting home. I've done my bit . . .'

'But, Joe,' said Randalf. 'Joe the Barbarian. There is one small matter . . .'

'Oh, yes, I was forgetting,' said Joe as he pulled the pouch of silver pipsqueaks from his pocket. 'The Horned Baron gave me this. It's my fee.' He held it out. 'You may as well have it. I won't be needing it where I'm going.'

'Oh, Joe,' said Randalf. 'Your bravery is unsurpassed, your ingenuity unequalled and now I find your generosity is also unmatched—and yet that was not the little matter to which I was referring.'

'Then, what is it?' said Joe. His heartbeat was beginning to race. 'I've kept my side of the bargain. Now it's time to keep yours. You *must* send me home.'

'I can't,' he said.

'Can't?' said Joe. 'What do you mean, *can't*?'

Randalf looked down. 'I mean, I can't,' he said.

'He's right, you know,' said Veronica. 'He wouldn't know where to start, I can vouch for that.'

Joe's stomach churned. His head spun. 'But . . . but you brought me here,' he said.

'I know,' said Randall. 'I used my warrior-hero-summoning spell,' he said. 'Unfortunately, it is the only spell I have to hand.'

'Yeah,' said Veronica scornfully, 'that's because all the other spells—including the warrior-hero-returning spell are . . .'

'Are elsewhere,' Randalf interrupted hurriedly.

'Can't you fetch it?' said Joe.

'I'm afraid not,' said Randalf.

'You mean to say, I'm stuck here!' said Joe indignantly.

'For the time being,' Randalf confirmed.

'No, no, I've got to get back . . .' said Joe. 'Why can't you *fetch* it?' he demanded. 'Why?'

'Because . . . because . . .' Randalf faltered.

'Go on, tell him,' said Veronica. 'You know where it is. After all, there's only one place it could be!'

'Where?' said Joe.

Randalf grimaced. 'Giggle Glade,' he said.

'Giggle Glade?' said Joe.

'It's in the middle of Elfwood,' said Randalf.

'Elfwood?' said Joe. Veronica had mentioned Elfwood before.

'It's the residence of . . .' He shuddered violently. 'Dr Cuddles.'

'Dr Cuddles . . .' said Joe slowly.

'Blimey,' said Veronica. 'He's more of a parrot than I am, and that's saying something for a budgie!'

'Dr Cuddles is . . . is the one who stole Roger the Wrinkled's *Great Book of Spells*,' Randalf confessed. 'He's been using it ever since. You remember the flying cupboards?'

'And the stampeding cutlery?' said Norbert.

Joe nodded. Randalf shuddered again.

'That was no doubt the work of Dr Cuddles,' he said. 'If anything goes wrong in Muddle Earth, you can bet your last pipsqueak, somewhere at the bottom of it all, you'll find Dr Cuddles of Giggle Glade!'

'That's it!' Veronica exclaimed.

'He's power mad!' said Randalf. 'He'll stop at nothing to take control of Muddle Earth and become its absolute ruler. And if that should ever happen,' he went on, 'then all the denizens of Muddle Earth would be forced to dance to his evil tune . . .'

'*That's it!*' squawked Veronica a second time.

'*What's* it?' said Randalf irritably.

'It wasn't Grubley who stole the ogre's snuggly-wuggly,' said Veronica. 'He was telling the truth when he said he obtained it from one of his contacts. The question is, who was that contact?'

Randalf shook his head. 'You don't mean . . .' he said.

Veronica tutted impatiently. 'Just think about it. Who stood to gain from Engelbert destroying the Horned Baron's castle in his rage?' she asked. 'Who would have welcomed a bit of argy-bargy between the goblins and the ogres? And where was Grubley coming from with that roll of singing material? Elfwood! And who lives in Elfwood?'

'Dr Cuddles,' said Randalf, Norbert

and Veronica in hushed unison. 'Stealing an ogre's snuggly-wuggly! What will he think of next!' They all shook their heads.

It was Joe who broke the long silence that followed. 'That's handy,' he said.

Randalf looked at him quizzically. 'Handy?' he said.

'You'll be able to find out when we pay him a visit to ask him to return the *Great Book of Spells*,' he said.

Randalf laughed nervously. 'Joe, my dear boy, nobody pays a visit to Giggle Glade. You can't just ask Dr Cuddles to return the spell book. That's what Roger the Wrinkled and the other wizards thought. "We'll discuss it over a nice pot of tea, Randalf," they said— and look what happened to them!'

'What?' said Joe.

'Well, I don't actually know,' admitted Randalf. 'But they didn't come back!'

Joe shrugged. 'If going to see Dr Cuddles of Giggle Glade is my only chance of returning home, then it's a risk I'm prepared to take. Besides,' he said, before Randalf—or Veronica—

could speak, 'you're forgetting something very important.'

'And what might that be?' asked Randalf.

Joe smiled. 'I am JOE THE BARBARIAN!' he proclaimed in his biggest voice.

'I . . . I know that,' said Randalf uncertainly. 'But . . .'

Trust me,' said Joe. 'I'm a warrior-hero.'

A chill wind whistled through the trees of Elfwood. The leaves rustled, the boughs creaked. At its very centre, the dappled light illuminating Giggle Glade was fading fast.

'We failed, master,' came the nasal voice of Dr Cuddles's assistant.

'Yes,' came the squeaky reply, followed by high-pitched giggles. 'We failed.'

'And we planned the singing curtains scam so well! The fake advertisement in the catalogue. The theft of

Engelbert the Enormous's snuggly-wuggly—ooh, those ogres can be *so* stupid! The haggling with that odious little goblin, Grubley . . . It was all going so well.'

'Yes,' Dr Cuddles giggled unpleasantly, 'by now, Muddle Earth should have been in chaos! And I would have been its ruler. I didn't think my old friend, Randalf the Apprentice, had it in him to use that spell a second time.' The sinister giggles grew louder. 'Curse that warrior-hero!'

'My thoughts entirely,' his assistant agreed.

'But our work shall continue. I shall devise an even better plan! One that cannot fail! I shall destroy the warrior-hero once and for all!' he shouted, each word interspersed with the hideous giggling. 'I shall conquer the Horned Baron!'

All round the clearing, the woodland creatures were troubled by the sound of the raised voice. As it reached its terrifying crescendo, stiltmice tottered, tree rabbits fell out of their trees, while the roosting batbirds—already wary after an attacking flock of cupboards had left them battered and uneasy—deserted their perches and flapped off across the sky.

'That all sounds absolutely super,' said his assistant. 'Now, how about a nice cup of tea and a snuggle-muffin. I've decorated one specially with your face . . .'

'What would I do without you, Quentin?' said Dr Cuddles. 'Now, I need to get down to my plan.' He stroked his chin. 'I must cover every angle. Allow for every possibility.' He looked up. 'I'm thinking dragons. I'm thinking mangel-wurzel marmalade. I'm thinking small, tinkly teaspoons . . .' He giggled and rubbed his hands together gleefully. 'It's going to be perfect, Quentin.'

'Ooh, you're so evil, master,' Quentin purred.

The giggles grew menacing. 'You haven't seen anything yet, believe me, Quentin,' he said. His voice (and giggles) became louder. 'And there is not a thing that Randalf, or anyone else, can do to stop me! I, DOCTOR

CUDDLES OF GIGGLE GLADE, SHALL BECOME LORD AND MASTER OF MUDDLE EARTH!!!' he roared, and he threw back his head in crazed triumph.

'*Tee-hee-hee-hee-hee-hee-hee-hee . . . !*'